THE GOSPEL ACCORDING TO

Gray Collins

A WE BURN BEAUTIFUL PREQUEL

LANCE LANSDALE

Copyright © 2025 by Lance Lansdale

All rights reserved.

No part of this publication may be reproduced, distributed, or transmitted in any form or by any means, including photocopying, recording, or other electronic or mechanical methods, without the prior written permission of the publisher, except as permitted by U.S. copyright law. For permission requests, contact Lance Lansdale.

The story, all names, characters, and incidents portrayed in this production are fictitious. No identification with actual persons (living or deceased), places, buildings, and products is intended or should be inferred.

Pirating is trash. Hope you cry, hope you die.

Cover art: Lance Lansdale (yaaas!)

Editing: Lindsay with the mermaid hair

Content Warning
(A CUTE FONT FOR A NOT-SO-CUTE TOPIC)

Religious trauma
On page homophobic assault
A man threatening a woman with physical violence
No sexual contact until eighteen
Domestic abuse (violence between husband and wife. Not on page, but bruising is noticeable, and it's briefly discussed)
Trevor Collins being the absolute fucking worst

No HEA or HFN until We Burn Beautiful

TO ANYONE WHO HAS EVER HAD TO HIDE THEIR SPARKLE.

Burn Beautiful

Contents

Chapter One	1
Chapter Two	10
Chapter Three	19
Chapter Four	44
Chapter Five	57
Chapter Six	72
Chapter Seven	98
Note From Lance	121
For More About Me	122

Chapter One

February 1998

In the beginning God created the heavens and the earth. Then he created Kent Fox. When he said *"Let there be light,"* I hadn't realized he'd meant the light that poured out of Kent directly at me. When he said *"Let us make mankind in our image,"* I realized just how stunning the Almighty actually was.

I was thirteen when the boy with tangled curls and big, brown, puppy-dog eyes joined my life's trajectory. He was confusion. Chaos. Consumption. Kent Fox enveloped me, wrapping himself around my life like Jesus' shroud. I am a man made of regrets, but Kent has *never* been one of them.

The schoolhouse wasn't like any schoolhouse I'd seen before. It was just a navy-blue home in a residential area. A repurposed three-bedroom house that was gutted and shaped into the image Brother Blankenship saw fit. That's what Momma told me, at least.

I hadn't understood why my parents called him Brother when we didn't know the man from Adam, but Daddy explained that in the evangelical community, it was just how things were done. Brothers and Sisters in Christ.

"Hands," my mother said as she rooted through her purse, looking for who knows what. We'd been standing on the porch for over five minutes, waiting for someone to answer the door. I asked her why, if it was a schoolhouse, we needed to knock. Rather than answer, she'd done what she often did—turned her attention away from me. Instead of a simple *'it's the polite thing to do, Grayson,'* she ignored me the same way she did with the nonbelievers who lived two doors down, back home in Arkansas. If she didn't acknowledge them, they didn't exist. And, in turn, if she didn't pay me a bit of attention, she could pretend *it* didn't exist. The little part of me that made me unworthy. Heck, I didn't even know what that part of me was, but it had always been there. This invisible wall that kept her at arm's length. She wasn't like that with my brother, Trevor. She doted on him like he was the king of England or something.

After another five minutes of uncomfortable silence, a woman appeared in the doorway, a smile cracked right across her face, bigger than any I'd ever seen before. It was warmth and sunshine and an overwhelming sense of joy.

The woman—Sister Thorpe, she called herself—traipsed through the home-turned-private school as if she were walking on air. Her high heels clacked against the floorboards, each step reverberating around us through the narrow hallway. Ahead of us, at the end of the hall, was an open doorway leading to what seemed to be a kitchen. To the left, two doors were open, and as we passed the first room, I spotted a pair of toddlers wandering around aimlessly. One was holding a crucifix molded out of Play-Doh, and the other held his hands in the air like he was praising God.

The next room housed the middle-schoolers. Inside, there was a woman in a long denim skirt sitting at a desk, reading a book. Makeshift cubicles lined the sides of the room, each cubby facing the wall. Despite the overwhelming number of desks in such a small space, there were only three school kids in the room. Two boys were at their desks, scribbling in workbooks, and there was a girl standing in front of a long, rectangular table in the middle of the room. She had two books in front of her and a red pen in her hand. I wasn't sure what she was doing, and I didn't get a chance to ask, because Sister Thorpe took my hand and led me toward the room on the right. Her hands felt like velvet against mine. Soft and warm, not like Momma's. Momma's felt like ice cubes most of the time.

Just like the classroom before, the door was open. As Sister Thorpe turned around and spoke with my mother about scripture, I peered inside. The room was just as big as the middle-schoolers', the main difference being the amount of students. Inside, roughly fifteen kids were sitting at their desks, and the only sound in the room was a CD boombox playing "Flower in the Rain" by Jaci Velasquez—one of my favorites.

The room was beige, both in color and in spirit. Crucifixes were spread across the walls, none of which seemed to be placed with care. A black cross that looked like it was made of iron was hanging low, right above a brunette girl's desk. For her sake, I hoped it had been securely fastened, because it looked heavy enough to crack her head wide open if it fell.

Sister Thorpe smiled down at me, waiting for an answer to a question I hadn't heard. I stalled, shoving my hands into my pockets again, just needing an outlet for the bumblebees buzzing around in my stomach.

Her smile seemed kind. Almost overly so. She pointed at an empty desk toward the back of the room. "Sugar, why don't you go in and get settled? We've got your workbooks ready; pens and pencils and the like. I just need to go over a few more things with your mother."

I turned toward my mother, seeking her approval. She had that look in her eyes. The one she had before we moved to West Clark, two weeks ago. There was anger and venom bubbling under the surface, waiting for me to make one wrong move. She had that look a lot, back before my parents sat my brother and me down and told us everything was going to be normal again. No more fighting. No more late nights at the dealership for Daddy. No more feeling like it was all my fault, even though I didn't know why.

"What do you say to Mrs. Thorpe, Gray?" Momma asked with a twist of annoyance coating the words.

"Thank you, Mrs.—I mean Sister Thorpe. I promise, I'm gonna be on my best behavior. I ain't gonna give you any trouble." I looked up at Momma, wanting to make sure she was happy with my answer, but she was turned toward the wall, staring at a framed drawing of Jesus one of the students must've done. In it, Jesus had these big blue eyes that almost seemed to be looking back at me—right into my soul.

Sister Thorpe leaned down, tapping the tip of my nose with her finger, and chuckled. "You're precious." She had a genuine smile on her face, like meeting me was the high point of her day. Her voice was soft and meek, with an almost childlike innocence to it. "Why don't you go and get settled at that desk in the back. Your neighbor isn't much of a morning person, so if he's in a bad mood, don't take it personally." Her finger tilted to the left, pointing at a boy who was slumped over his desk with his head down. She was staring at me, but she aimed her next question at my mother. "Has your family settled on a church home yet?"

Momma opened her checkbook and clicked the tip of her pen before scribbling across the paper. Without looking up, she said, "Martin took us to Harmony Methodist last Sunday, but we've always been Baptists."

Sister Thorpe gasped, and if she'd been wearing pearls, I was sure she would've been clutching them. "Oh, sweetie, no. Now, I'm not generally one to push their beliefs on others, but that's a line I'm going to have to cross today." She flicked her wrist toward the classroom and smiled down at me, ushering me forward. I smiled back, because she seemed like a really nice lady. As I made my way in, I overheard her telling my mother about a man named Reverend Thomas who had just been caught doing something called 'fornicating' with the church secretary. I'd heard that word before, back when we were still in Arkansas. For the Reverend's sake, I hoped his wife hadn't cut up all his clothes the same way Momma had with Daddy's.

Inside the room, the atmosphere felt robotic. Each child was facing the wall, sitting in those same cubicles I'd seen in the other room. The desks, it seemed, were just really long planks of plywood secured to the wall with a nail and a prayer. On each side, there were wooden dividers separating students from their neighbors. Some were painted dark mahogany while others looked like cheap, unvarnished knotty-pine slats.

The desk she told me to sit at was in the very corner of the room, toward the back. There was another empty desk toward the front, and I guessed that's where my brother would be sitting when he got over his cold.

The boy sitting at the desk next to mine seemed to be the only person in the room who wasn't taking the work seriously. As the rest of the class scribbled away in colorful workbooks, he had his arms folded in front of him on the desk, resting his head on them like he was napping. His fingertips tapped the cheap particle board desk, the beat sounding practiced and familiar. I'd heard it before, but I couldn't place it.

I walked to my new desk and set my backpack on the floor next to my chair, but the boy in the seat beside me didn't budge. Not when I sat in my chair. Not as I explored the items left for me on the desk. Not even when I wheeled my chair back, turned to him, and said, "Hi. I'm Gray. Well, Grayson, but everyone just calls me Gray." All that earned me was a slightly raised arm and a halfhearted wave. He wasn't even looking up at me. "We just moved here from Little Rock," I continued, hoping that might get him talking, but he just groaned. "Daddy cashed in his ... I think he called it a forty-one-k, and he used the money to buy our new farm."

He lifted his hand and daintily twinkled his fingers like he was shooing me away. That probably should have been the point where I gave up and stared quietly into my cubicle until Sister Thorpe explained what I was supposed to be doing. Unfortunately, my mouth moved on autopilot most of the time. Add in my jittery nerves and the stress of not knowing anyone, and it was a recipe for unfiltered chaos. I couldn't have stopped myself if I tried.

"Daddy's raising sheep. Says he can sell off their hair. I didn't know people bought sheep hair. Did you? Momma says he ain't got any business running a farm after the way he ran the dealership into the ground back home. They were fighting a lot before we moved. She said this would be like a fresh start. Back to the way things used to be—but I don't know."

He groaned again, pressing his forehead even deeper into the crook of his elbow.

"I like your hair," I said, just trying to get some sort of reaction. An acknowledgment. A nod. Maybe even a smile. "Do you always talk so much?"

"Listen," he said without looking up, "I'm sure you're a fantastic guy, and I'm more than happy to listen to you ramble about things I don't particularly care about, but I'm going to need you to take it down about twenty-seven notches. It is *far* too early, and I'm absolutely useless before noon." He sat up in his chair and turned toward me. His mouth was open, like he was getting ready to unload more of that sass on me, but when our eyes met, he took in a quick breath. His eyes widened like he'd just learned all the secrets of the universe. I wanted him to share each and every one of them with me.

"Sorry. I know—I mean, I can be ..." I cleared my throat. Gosh, his eyes sure were brown. Little orbs of chocolatey goodness.

"No! *I'm* sorry," he said with more force than the situation called for. His head was shaking back and forth so fast I thought it might just spin around in a circle. "I wasn't trying to be rude." He raked his fingers through the mound of dark brown curls on his head. "I'm Kent. Hey—yeah—Kent. Hi there. You said your name was Gray?" He shoved his hand forward, and for a second, I thought he was going to slap me, but he just held it there. His cheeks were a little redder than they had been when he first sat up, but I chalked that up to the fact it was triple digits outside, and whoever was in charge of the air conditioning must have been frugal as all get out, because it wasn't much cooler inside than it was out. I just sat there with a funny feeling inside of me, my heart racing as he scooted closer and took my hand in his, giving it a shake.

Gosh. This guy. Pale skin, a light dusting of freckles across his nose and cheeks. He was so fascinating! I felt like I could have studied him for years and still find new details, decades down the line.

I licked my lips because they were feeling a little too dry for my liking. "Hey there. Gray. Gray Collins. Hi, Kent. Hey." For a moment, I worried I might be having one of those strokes like Nana Collins had a few years back. Momma said she'd started talking gibberish and her eye was twitching *'like a son of a gun'* before Nana passed out.

Are strokes contagious? Can you catch them years after the fact? And what the heck is the deal with this kid's eyes? Gosh, they're neat.

"Hey," he said again, still stuck in the relentless whirlpool of words we were both swept up in. The girl in the seat behind Kent leaned back in her chair and stared at me, one eyebrow lifted in accusation.

"Are you two okay?" She cocked her head to the side and stared at me like I was diseased. Her eyes shifted back and forth between my hand and my face. She rolled her eyes and turned back around in her chair. Kent, though ... He must have thought I was going in for a hug, because he gasped, and then his arms were around me, his hand patting me on the back, offering me a side-hug.

Explosions. That's what his hug held. Little bursts of sunshine and sparkles.

"Go to Hell, Kate," he growled, not taking his eyes off me. "Have you ever gone to a private school before, Gray?" Kent asked, leaning back in his chair.

"No. Momma said I'd probably fare better in one. Said the kids might be a little nicer if they were being raised right. I didn't have a lot of friends back in Arkansas."

He laughed, light and low. Shame flooded my cheeks because it felt like he was laughing at me. Like I'd just made some big blunder, ruining any chance of a possible friendship. I clasped my hands together, leaning forward, putting my weight on my arms against my knees, unable to look him in the eyes.

"Hey," he said, rolling his chair toward me. "What's wrong?"

I shook my head. "Nothing. It's just ... I have a habit of embarrassing myself." Slowly, I peeked up at him, trying to force a smile. "I probably shouldn't have told you about me not having any friends."

"I wasn't laughing because you didn't have any friends, goofy." He reached forward, tussling my hair. I flinched at the uninvited touch, but the smile he was giving me melted away all the ice running through my veins. "I just thought it was cute how call your mother 'Momma'." Our eyes locked, and we stared at each other long enough that I got a little uncomfortable. He must have sensed it, because he sat up straight and wheeled his chair closer, pointing at something on the desk. I turned to see what he was trying to show me.

The desk was a confusing mess of trinkets and booklets. There was a small black flag stand with two flags poking out of it. A miniature Christian flag, and a mini-Old Faithful. Next to the desk-sized flags, there was a stack of four workbooks. Kent reached for them, spreading them across the table.

"Here," he said with a grin. The books weren't very big. Maybe sixty or seventy pages each. There were ones for math, English, social studies, and science. Fanning the pages of one book, Kent explained, "We work at your own pace. You read through the workbooks, and then there are little quizzes. When you're done with the quizzes, you raise your flag."

"Raise my flag?"

He nodded, pointing at the flag stand. "The Christian flag is for when you're stuck on a question and you need Sister Thorpe's help." He peered back at the doorway. Momma and Sister Thorpe still hadn't come back, and Kent breathed out like he was relieved. "If you have a question, you should probably just ask me. Sister Thorpe's nice enough, but she doesn't know the first thing about math or English. Science neither."

"But she's our teacher, isn't she?"

He laughed so hard he snorted, slapping his hand against his thigh. When he composed himself, he just sat there smiling at me. "Supervisor. She's our supervisor."

"Like at a job?"

"If sitting in a little cubicle and pretending to do your work is a job, then yeah. Like at a job."

"But what if someone doesn't understand something? They can't all just come to you looking for help."

The girl poked her head out from behind Kent. "We all help each other out. If Kent doesn't know something, he'll ask me. If I don't know something, I'll ask Kyle." She turned around and stared at a portly boy on the other side of the room. "Don't ask him though. That's Tommy. He's a real jerk sometimes."

"It's true," Kent agreed. When I turned to face him, his eyes were still locked on me. Heat flooded my cheeks, and for the life of me, I couldn't figure out why I kept feeling so embarrassed in front of him. "And thank you, Kate," he said without looking back. "I don't remember asking for your input, but it sure is nice to know you're hanging onto my every word."

She snorted. "Screw you, dude."

My eyes must have doubled in size. I hadn't expected her to start talking like a sailor.

"Anyway ..." He rolled his eyes and pointed at the flags. "When you finish a quiz, you raise your American flag. That's to let Sister Thorpe know you're ready to grade your work."

"And she just comes over and takes the book?"

He shook his head. Swiveling his chair around, he turned and pointed at the big, long desk behind us. It was the same kind as the one the kid was using in the other room. "There's answer keys in the drawers there, and they're all labeled. You just take that booklet and match it up with your work book and grade yourself. If you get something wrong, you mark it with one of those red ink pens so you can bring your book back to your desk and fix it."

How the heck was that considered teaching?

"So, she doesn't actually teach us anything?"

Kent shook his head. "Work at your own pace, like I said."

"What's to stop me from taking one of those answer keys back to my desk and just filling it out for myself?"

Kent reached back toward his desk, pulling out a small, black and white booklet from under his mountain of workbooks. It was a math book, and across the top it said, ANSWER KEY.

My jaw almost hit the floor. "But that's cheating!"

He bumped his shoulder against mine and wiggled his eyebrows. "You catch on quick, Gray Collins." Leaning in even closer, he whispered, "I'll have you cheating right along with me, just you wait and see." His fingers threaded through my hair again, and he tapped the back of my head, right at the top, for some reason. "Can't wait to dirty you up."

Chapter Two

April 1998

Two months after meeting Kent, he invited me and my family to his church. Momma and Daddy decided to stick with Harmony Methodist for the time being, but she still offered to drop me off that evening.

Kent warned me that it could be kind of scary at first, but he assured me I didn't need to worry because he'd stick to me like glue. We made it to West Clark Apostolic Chapel a little before five that evening. Kent was sitting on the steps as music boomed out behind the closed double doors. The second he saw me, his eyes went wide and a smile stretched across his face. He stood up, brushing the dirt off his butt before he made his way toward us, his arm extended and aimed at me. I reached out and took it, my stomach doing a little spin under my skin as I touched a hand that was just pressed up against his butt. I probably should have been grossed out by it, but I wasn't.

Music swelled in the small chapel behind him, and inside men and women's shouts and hollering surpassed the sound of music. Loud chanting and shouts of 'hallelujah' reverberated inside the chapel walls, dripping through the crack and crevices of the old wooden building. I glanced down at the new watch Daddy got me the day we moved to West Clark. Ten 'til five.

"Are we late? I thought you said it didn't start until six?"

"You're good, dude. Service doesn't start until then, but people get here early to get their praise on." He lifted his hands and twinkled his fingers in an elaborate take on jazz hands. "So, are you ready to see the freakshow?"

"Freakshow?"

He snickered as he grabbed my wrist and pulled me toward the entrance, stopping when we were at the door and plopping down on the steps. I took a set beside him. "If you haven't been to an Apostolic church, this might be a lot for you. Just try to prepare yourself. If you get scared, or if it's too much, let me know and I can sneak you out when they start dancing down the aisle."

I lifted an eyebrow. "Dancing down the aisles?"

"Yeah, it's … It's hard to explain without seeing it for yourself. When we visit my Aunt Jeanie down in Tyler, we go to her Catholic church. It's a lot less energetic, and they do a lot of kneeling and standing and sitting." He let out an exasperated sigh and touched the back of his hand to his forehead like he was pretending he might faint. "All that up, down, up, down is far too much exercise for my liking."

I laughed so hard I snorted, and the corners of his lips curled up, then parted. His pretty white teeth were big, like they could chew up the entire world if he tried. I kind of wanted him to. For him to just chew up the whole dang universe until all that was left was him and me and that old rickety porch.

"I promise, if it's too much, we'll leave. I already told my dad you've never been to a church like this one. He says as long as we spend the time we would've been in service talking about God, it's okay. We just have to be quick about it so the other kids don't catch on."

I gave him a nod. "I'm fine."

"You say that now. Wait until you see Mr. Bronson running the pews."

"Running the pews?"

He waggled his eyebrows at me as if he'd just told some big joke I should have known the meaning of. Hanging his arm around my shoulder, he pulled me in for a side hug. I didn't understand the tingling sensation his touch sent down my back. Even worse, I didn't really understand the feeling of emptiness inside of me when he pulled away.

He stood and held his hand out for me. He must have hoisted me with a little too much force, because his pull sent me reeling. I crashed against him, blushing as he chuckled into my ear. "You alright, buddy?"

"I'm good." I pulled away and gave him a smile.

"Remember," he said as he made his way toward the door. "If you freak out, it's okay. Just let me know and we'll get out of here."

Bright red carpet lined the floors of the chapel. It wasn't a particularly large room, just an aisle separating two rows of pews. At the front was a small stage with two chairs that looked like thrones, both lined with red cushions and gold trim. A man and a lady were sitting in them, neither paying the other person much attention at all. I recognized the lady as Kent's mom from the times she'd picked him up from school. She'd been a kind woman with a sweet, almost baby-like voice. When she spoke, her words were hushed and timid; a stark contrast to my own mother's hollering.

She looked out into the crowd and our eyes met. Waving her arm like she was hailing a taxi, she flagged us down, calling us to the front. Kent led the way, and as he did a woman made her way out of the pew and into the aisle, digging through her purse. When her hand emerged, she was holding two small pieces of candy. They were those strawberry hard candies with the gooey center. Momma never let me have a lot of candy because she hated taking me to the dentist any more that she had to, so it was a rare treat when I got to snack on strawberry bon-bons.

The woman's hair was styled in an updo, her mountain of curls beaten into submission with hairspray. The hair was so stiff it looked like you could break the strands in half with ease. She wore a modest white blouse with cherry blossoms spreading up, down, and around her waist. The small neon-green purse she carried didn't match a single thing she was wearing, but I just chalked that up to her being old and her eyesight not being what it once was. She must have gotten dressed in the dark.

"You got yourself a new friend there, Kent?" she said, pointing at me.

Kent grabbed the little strawberry bon-bons and handed one to me before throwing his arm over my shoulder. "I sure do. His name's Gray Collins. He and his family moved here a few months back, from Little Rock. His daddy bought a farm outside of town and he's been raising sheep." He knocked his elbow against my arm. "Says they're selling their hair off to the highest bidder."

I blushed when I realized Kent must have hung on my every word when we were at school. He remembered all of it. I remembered his favorite things, too, but it was still a shock to know that he cared enough to pay attention to my ramblings.

She turned her attention to me, flashing me a smile. "Well it's awfully nice to meet you, Gray. I'm Sister Clifton."

"Nice to meet you, Sister," I said. I still didn't really understand the whole Brother-Sister thing these people kept insisting on, but I figured it was easier to roll with it than question them.

"So, Little Rock? I have a son out that way. He goes to North Point Pentecostal. Is that where your family went before you moved?" She eyed me with intensity, leaving me uncomfortable and with an overall sense of unease.

"No ma'am. We were Baptists."

Her eyes widened and she slowly backed her way into the pew, staring at me like I was diseased. "Well, that ... That sure is swell." Her eyes journeyed up and down, face to feet and then back again. "Glad we got to you in time." She took her seat and conversed with the women at her side.

I leaned over and whispered into Kent's ear, "What the heck was that about?"

"Don't worry about her. Don't worry about any of them, really," he said, pointing at the other ladies in the pew beside her. The other three ladies made no effort to get out of the pew—probably because Sister Clifton's knobby knees were blocking the way—but their gazes were all fixed on me.

The woman next to Sister Clifton waved at me. She was a heavyset Black woman. She was wearing a really pretty pink dress, but it didn't fit in with the styles of the other ladies in the pew; a bit more modern than the uniform black skirts and soft blouses.

"That's Ms. Dottie," Kent said, smiling adoringly at her. "She's my favorite." He waved his hand and beamed brightly like he was proud to be showing me off to all the people in his life, and it made my heart flutter with some strange new feeling I couldn't name.

"Ain't she a 'Sister', too?"

He shook his head. "She's never gone by Sister Pruitt. She's always just been Ms. Dottie to me." He waved even faster, getting her attention. "Hi, Ms. Dottie! This is my new friend, Gray."

Ms. Dottie returned Kent's wave. "Any friend of Kent's is a friend of mine, baby," she said with a stunning slow Southern drawl. "We'll have to chat later."

Their perfumes merged into a terrible foggy fragrance that smelled more like bug spray than something you'd buy at the department stores downtown. None of the women offered me their names, but that was mainly due to the happenings on stage. The ladies were enthralled with the piano player who was tinkering away, playing *The Old Rugged Cross*.

Kent led me to the second row of pews, taking his seat on the far end and patting the empty space beside him. On stage, Kent's father stood from his red and gold throne and walked to the podium.

His sermon wasn't like any sermon I'd ever heard before. The man wandered aimlessly around the stage, shouting so loudly into the microphone that spit was flying past, illuminated by the unnecessary spotlight aimed at him. As he harped on about blasphemy and people being ungrateful for the gifts God had given them, I turned to Kent. He was completely zoned out, staring at the back of the pew with a far-away look in his eyes. I watched him for a while. He almost seemed like he was in a trance. His fingers drew shapes and figures on the legs of his slacks, and a few times it almost looked like he'd been doodling hearts into the fabric. Without thinking, I reached over and drew one right above his knee. I must have tickled him, because he giggled before tapping the top of my hand with his finger. He traced a K against my skin like he was branding himself into my flesh. I could almost feel the fiery heat sizzling on my skin.

The music kicked in a little while after; a strong beat with blaring guitars accompanying. Sister Fox stood and made her way to the center of the stage, taking the microphone from Kent's daddy. She sang a song about shackles coming off her feet so that she could dance, and as she did, half the congregation stood and did just that. A stampede of men and women flooded the aisles and made their way to the front of the church, dancing like nobody was watching. Sister Clifton clicked her heels a few times, swaying her hips side to side as she reached for the sky. Beside her, a woman with blonde hair and a stuffy attitude shuffled modestly to the beat, looking uncomfortable, like she was only taking part due to obligation. The other two women who'd been sitting next to her in the pews, Ms. Dottie and Sister Thorpe, shimmied around, singing every line right along with Sister Fox.

A man zoomed down the aisle, and for a second, I thought there had been an emergency. I worried someone was choking or having a heart attack and he was trying to alert the pastor. When he reached the end of the aisle, he hopped up on the pew right beside Kent. Kent turned and stared at me, rolling his eyes.

"What?" I whispered.

"Just wait. You'll see."

The man was facing the back of the church, and he hiked one leg up, resting his foot on the back of the pew. I grabbed Kent's hand and squeezed.

"He's going to run the pews," Kent pointed out. "He always does it. It's the one interesting thing about him."

"I heard that, young man," the gentleman said.

"And I'll say it again," Kent bit back. "It's the only interesting thing about you." The man stared at the wall ahead, his fingers twitching with nerves. Kent leaned closer and brought his voice to a whisper, his breath tickling my ear. "This is the part where he acts like a total drama queen for five minutes before finally doing it, once everyone's looking. My mom says he's a narcissist."

"He's gonna fall."

"I wish," Kent said with a snort. He darted his eyes back at the man who was still staring ahead, like he was trying to work up the nerve to do something. Eventually, he smiled down at Kent and gave him a nod. The man hoisted himself up on the back of the pew ... and then he ran. He hopped and hopped, his feet touching down on each of the pews' backings without fault. When he reached the final one, he stood on the ball of his heel and twirled around like a ballerina. Hop after hop, he landed with ease until he finally reached our pew again. When he jumped forward and landed, he clapped his hands in the air, and then he danced right alongside Sister Thorpe.

Kent grabbed my wrist and gave me a look I couldn't quite read. "Are you okay?" he mouthed.

I leaned in and pressed my mouth against his ear. "I'm fine."

"Do you want to go outside anyway?" He must have known I was freaking out. I'd never seen anything like it in my life. All around, people were losing themselves to the music, and it scared the heck out of me. Kent looked up at his dad with a quirked eyebrow. Pastor Fox nodded, motioning toward the chapel doors. I gave Kent's dad an apologetic smile, but he mouthed that it was okay, and I could tell that he meant it.

We walked around the back of the church to the small, and into a large fenced-in yard. There were picnic tables all throughout, and Kent mentioned that they sometimes used them for potlucks like the ones we had at school on Fridays.

We headed toward the farthest table from the chapel, way out by the fence. The grass was overgrown like no one had thought to mow it all summer. I was on the stool, but Kent hoisted himself up and sat on top of the table, his feet right beside me.

"So, we have to talk about God?" I asked.

"If you want," he said with a shrug. Kent didn't really seem to take religion seriously, I'd noticed. I didn't know if it was down to him resenting being born into it, or if he just really didn't believe. I didn't want to think about him not believing and maybe ending up in Hell when this life was over.

"That music was really pretty. The dancing was kind of scary, but the songs were beautiful. We didn't have that back home. It was just a piano and Mrs. Maverick singing off-key hymns."

"Sounds dreadful," he said, tracing circles across the table with his fingers. "I like the slower songs. People usually stand still and pray during them. I always feel like Mom and Dad expect me to be front and center, dancing with everyone else. It's nice to just relax, you know?"

"You shouldn't have to do anything you don't want to."

"I know. But I'm the pastor's son. It's expected."

I laid my head against his thigh, my face inches from his stomach. "I bet you dance good."

He blushed. "I have my moments."

I tapped his thigh and traced circles into his slacks, the same way he'd done to the table earlier. Kent reached down and ran his fingers through my hair. We didn't say anything for a while. We just stared at each other. Everyone I knew—Momma, Daddy, Trevor—they were never comfortable with the quiet. They talked in circles just to fill the empty space, but sometimes, I just wanted to *be* without having to perform. I'd get nervous sometimes, trying to think of topics to keep the conversation flowing, but I never felt that way with Kent. It was like he *got* me. He understood, because he was the same.

Eventually, I broke the silence. "I sing sometimes."

"Yeah?"

"Momma says I have a pretty voice, but she's my mother. I think she has to say that."

His fingers tugged my hair, gentle, but enough for me to feel him. "You can sing for me if you'd like. I'll tell you if you're good."

"I don't know," I said, dropping my gaze back to his shirt. I wished I hadn't brought the subject up. There was something about putting myself out there, opening myself up to his judgment, that sent a wave of panic crashing through me. "You might laugh."

"I wouldn't." His fingers scratched my scalp. "Promise. Go on. I want to hear you."

"Right now?"

"It's okay," he said. "You don't have to if you don't want to, but I'd love to hear what you sound like."

I closed my eyes, letting myself get lost in the feeling of his fingers running through my hair. The gentle massage cracked me open like an egg, letting out all of the parts I kept hidden from the rest of the world.

"Is there any song in particular that you want to hear?"

"Nah. Just something for me."

For Kent. A song meant just for him. I racked my brain trying to think of one. There was *Lord I Lift Your Name on High*, which was poppy and a little sassy. It was in tune with who Kent was as a person, but it didn't feel right. *Glorify Thy Name* would have been a good choice. I'd have glorified Kent's name any day. Still, it wasn't *him*.

I pictured him in my mind. I imagined him as a grown up, blasting through life like the ringleader at a circus, all passion and flair and over-the-top antics. I could see him so clearly in my mind. All that power and charisma overflowing like communion wine. The funny thing was, I could picture myself right there beside him. Smiling over at him like he held the whole world in his hands. My life hadn't had a bit of purpose until we moved to West Clark. It was almost like it only took form and unfolded the day I met him. He was my beginning, and I was pretty sure I wanted him to be there with me right up through the end. In life. In death. Right by my side.

I slid my hand over his, holding it closer to my scalp, and then I sang.

"*Abide with me,*" I began.

Every word—every single lyric—felt like it had been written about him and me. Life would be hard for me. I didn't know why, but I felt it deep down in the pit of my stomach. I knew if he was there, standing right beside me, I could face it all with pride. When the world was dark and cold and lonely, he'd make it all better. When the outside world held little to no interest to me, he'd be all the interest I needed. That was the song. That was *his* song.

When I looked up at him, his eyes were a little misty, and he was staring at me with such intensity, I didn't know how long I could stand it.

"Just for you, Kent," I whispered. "Just for you."

Chapter Three

June 1998

"I want you to be on your best behavior, Grayson," my mother said as she pulled into the Fox family's driveway. Putting the car into park, she turned and kissed my forehead before combing her fingers through my hair.

"Yeah, Grayson," my brother teased from the back seat. "Be on your best behavior."

Momma turned and glared at him. "That's enough of that. You're already in trouble for sassing Sister Thorpe at school."

Trevor rolled his eyes. "That's the whole reason I'm stuck at home with you while Gray gets to go queer it up with his stupid queer friend."

Momma narrowed her eyes at him, but I didn't know what the word meant. I'd heard Trevor say it a few times, and he usually used it when he was talking about someone he didn't like, so I just assumed it was another way of calling someone dumb.

Momma looked like she was ready to wash his mouth out with soap. "Don't ever say that word again," she snapped. "Not in front of Grayson. He's at a delicate age. Do you hear me?" It was the angriest I'd ever heard her. Even angrier than the night she cut the crotch out of all Daddy's dress pants. "Answer me, young man."

When I saw my brother in the rearview mirror, he looked smaller than I'd ever seen him. It was like he was trying to fold in on himself. I'd seen Trev scare folks off with just a dirty look, but in the back seat, his hands clasped politely in his lap, too nervous to get a word out, he looked a lot like me. I never saw much of a resemblance in us before. While he was all muscles and tan skin and pearly white teeth, I was made up of lanky limbs and gapped teeth and a butt as big as Dallas.

"I'm sorry," he whispered before turning to me. "I'm sorry, Gray." The look of rage he normally shot me was nonexistent. He was staring at me like he meant it. Considering I had no idea what the heck he'd even called me, the whole situation made me nervous.

"Momma?"

She turned and smiled at me. A real smile. "Yes?"

"What's a queer?"

She grabbed the steering wheel and squeezed until her knuckles went white. She closed her eyes and took a deep breath, exhaling slowly. "Are you excited about your sleepover?" When she opened her eyes, she plastered a smile across her face. "You boys are going to have a wonderful time." The way she switched her emotions so quickly left me feeling a little dizzy.

"Yes, ma'am."

I looked out the window. Kent Fox was right there. Right inside that house. We were going to spend the whole night together. I was going to have him all to myself. No nosy Kate poking her head into our A and B conversations that she refused to C her way out of. No stinky Kyle coming over to poke Kent in the ribs while we were talking. Not even Sister Thorpe checking on our work, asking us if we needed help, only to blubber out a bunch of nonsense when she didn't know the answer. Just him and me.

"If Mrs. Fox tells you to do something, I want you to do it. No backtalk. Understood?"

I nodded, trying my best to keep my excitement contained. "Promise!"

"You must really like this Kent."

"He's great. You'd love him. Maybe we could have him over one night, too. Since he's letting me spend the night with him, it only seems right."

I wanted Kent to come to my house, so I could show him my room and all the stuff in it. We'd become inseparable at school, taking our breaks and lunches together, sharing ziplocked Pringles and Fruit Stripe gum. I wanted to show him everything in my room because I wanted him to know me. To really *know* me. What I liked and what I didn't. All my interests. I'd have to hide the stuffed animals so he didn't think I was still a big old baby who needed his elephant to fall asleep. I'd also need to tuck my pink Hot Wheels car under my mattress so he didn't ask me why I liked girl colors. Honestly, I didn't really think he'd mind. In the four months we'd known each other, he'd never made fun of me. Not in a cruel way, at least. Sure, he joked about my freckles and would pinch my stomach and mention how skinny I was, but the big things—the small gap between my front teeth, the way my butt was bigger than the other boys at school, how I sometimes had to ask Sister Thorpe stupid questions about schoolwork that I should already have known, even though she didn't know, either—he never joked about any of that. And the same way he didn't laugh at me, I never laughed at him. Not when the boys in class would make frilly hand gestures, or when Kent would be leaning over in his chair and Tommy would sneak up and grab his chest, pretending like Kent had boobs because he was a little heavy. I would never make fun of him for that. I didn't care that he had a tummy or how his cheeks were a little puffy. I thought he looked nice the way he was. He always looked real nice.

"If you need me, you'll call," Momma said with a serious face. "I'll come right over and get you."

I leaned over the center console and crushed her with a hug, smashing a kiss to her cheek. "Promise! Can I go now?" I bounced in my seat again, unable to contain my excitement. Momma just laughed and nodded, reaching across me and unlocking the door.

"Go ahead. I want you to call me tonight, even if you don't need me to pick you up."

"Promise!" I opened the door and stepped out of the car. I grabbed the door but paused. Leaning down, smiled at her. "Thanks for letting me spend the night."

She seemed taken aback, like she hadn't expected it. "You're welcome, Grayson."

"Love you. I'll tell you all about it when I get home."

She chuckled. "I love you too. Now, go on. And be a good boy for Mr. and Mrs. Fox."

I slammed the door and spun around, racing toward their house. It was a really pretty house, too. There were only three homes in the cul-de-sac, and the Fox's easily had the nicest. It was a tan two-story home with a garage to the side. They had a wrap-around porch, just like us, and there were rose bushes in front of it. I made a mental note to tell Momma we ought to plant some at our house because of how pretty they were.

Three steps and a porch were all that stood between me, Kent Fox, and "a night I'd never forget," as he'd sold it to me. He didn't have to sell me on anything, though. I knew it would be a blast. It was my first night away from home, and I was spending it with my best friend. Of course, I'd never forget it.

I hopped the stairs and rushed forward. Before I could knock, the wooden door opened, and there he was, like he'd been watching out the window, waiting for me.

Kent looked even nicer than usual. At school, we all wore the same uniform; khakis and tucked-in Polo shirts. At church, we wore button-downs and slacks. But there, in his sanctuary, Kent Fox was an explosion of expression. He had on a blue shirt with a giant pink flamingo across the front, its neck craned to the side, beak open. From where it was placed on the shirt, it almost looked like the little guy was trying to bite Kent's nipple off. His shorts were sky-blue, and they looked tight. Tighter than I'd ever be comfortable wearing, at least. His sloppy curls had actually been styled for once. He had them shoved to the side and they seemed to have been doused in hair product to keep them locked in place. I'd never been a fan of hair gel, but if it could make me look half as nice as Kent did, I'd slather it in my hair every day for the rest of my life.

Kent was bouncing up and down on his toes, just like me. I wasn't sure if he'd been that amped up before I got there, or if my excitement was contagious, but it didn't matter either way. He hopped forward, wrapping his arms around me and pulling me in for a crushing hug. It was our first chest-to-chest hug.

Up until then, we'd only ever shared side hugs. It made my skin tingle like little angels were tiptoeing up and down my arms.

"Hey, Gray. Hey there. How's it hanging?"

"Kent. Hi. Hi there. Good. It's good. So good," I answered, crushing him right back.

"I've got so much stuff I want to show you. I have the whole night planned."

"You do?"

He broke the hug and pulled away, but I kind of wanted him to keep hugging me. "I've been planning it for days."

He'd been thinking about me for days. Obsessing over making this the perfect night. I wanted it to be perfect, too, because I wanted to be worth all his effort.

"Come on," he said. "Mom can't wait to see you. She keeps telling me we're all playing board games in the living room tonight, but we'll see about that."

"I like board games," I argued. "I don't mind."

He shook his head. "Dad's going to be home after supper."

"Your Dad's nice."

"My dad is a jerk. Trust me, we'll have a lot more fun if it's just us. He'll just yammer on about fire and brimstone, and we'll never hear the end of it. I've never had a friend stay the night with me before. I just want it to be special, you know?" As his cheeks flushed with color, he looked away. "Sorry. I know that probably makes me sound like a loser."

"It's my first sleepover, too," I blurted, just wanting to put him at ease. "I didn't have a lot of friends back home." Any. I didn't have any friends back home. "If you want it to be just you and me, then that's what we'll do."

He smiled. Just the slightest twitch of his lip. "Just you and me." He led me inside, and as I crossed the threshold, I took in my surroundings. Their house was just as pretty on the inside as it was on the outside. The front door opened into a foyer. On the left, an archway led to the living room, and to the right, there was a staircase with another small hallway beside it. Kent pointed down the hall, toward two closed doors.

"That's Dad's office, and the next door down is their bedroom."

"Where's yours?"

He pointed at the staircase. "I've got the whole second floor to myself."

My eyes bulged. "The whole floor?"

"The whole floor. It's gonna be just you and me up there," he said, waggling his eyebrows like a goofball. "My room's right on top of theirs, so if we stay up past my bedtime, we can't walk around or they'll hear us. We can just lay in bed and talk, though." He flashed me a smile and squeezed my wrist.

"I like talking to you," I blurted. Once the words were out, I cringed. Gosh. I sounded like such a weirdo.

He leaned forward until our foreheads were almost touching. Then he thumped my nose. "I know," he whispered. "I like talking to you, too."

Yanking me forward by the wrist, he led me into the living room. There was a couch on the left with an ugly floral print. In front of it, there was a cheap coffee table that looked like it had been painted to look fancier than it really was. A giant picture window was behind the couch, and the curtains were drawn, letting light blast through the glass, illuminating the room. On the far wall, there was a fireplace, and beside it, a small TV with a VHS player on top. Crucifixes were hung all over the place, and no matter which way I turned, it was like Jesus was staring down at me. It was nice. It made me feel safe. When I turned to Kent, he winced.

"Sorry. I know it's a lot. Mom and Dad don't hold anything back when it comes to God."

I just smiled at him, wanting to put him at ease. "I like it. It feels like He's all around us."

Kent just stared past me and sighed. "Yeah." He kicked his foot against the hardwood floor and stared down at his shoes. "It gets old, though. Sometimes it feels like my entire life is wrapped up in religion. I just want to ... *be. Y*ou know? Without God staring down and judging me all the time."

I didn't know what to say to that. I'd never heard anyone be so dismissive of God. It made me nervous, like God might throw a lightning bolt down at us. I covered his mouth with my hand. He arched an eyebrow at me but I shook my head.

"Don't talk like that." I darted my eyes up at the ceiling. "He's always listening."

Kent chuckled, gently grabbing my wrist and pulling my hand away from his face. "Let Him listen, then."

I looked at the television set. "Sister Thorpe said Apostolics don't watch television."

"Dad has our church secretary record his sermons. He rewatches them a lot—usually one a night. Sometimes he makes me watch with him, which, ugh, the worst. He says he does it to improve his sermons, but I think he just likes to hear himself talk." He squeezed my wrist and tugged. "Come on. Let's say hey to Mom and then we can head upstairs." He led me through the archway to our right, into the kitchen. Mrs. Fox was standing over the sink peeling potatoes, and she was humming a familiar hymn.

"Gray's here," Kent said, walking to the refrigerator and pulling out two cans of Sprite. He tossed one to me and I caught it, thankfully. I'd never been too good at sports, and busting a soda can all over Mrs. Fox's spotless kitchen floor probably wouldn't have been the best first impression. Granted, we'd seen each other pretty often when she came to pick Kent up from school, but still. I didn't want her to think I was a bad guest.

Mrs. Fox turned around and gave me a warm, welcoming smile. Her hair was the same as it had been at church. A frizzy hill of hair, held in pace by who knows how many bobby pins. She was dressed head-to-toe in denim. Denim skirt. Denim jacket. Her blouse looked like it was cotton, but it was still that same dark blue shade with white spatters all over the fabric. She had a small bruise under her eye which looked a little painful. I could smell her perfume from the other side of the kitchen, a pretty scent, but it seemed like something an older woman would wear, like those ladies Kent introduced me to at church. We'd seen them around town, always dressed head to toe in denim, hair piled high, jacked up to Jesus.

The Denim Debutantes, I'd named them one Tuesday in the lunchroom. Kent got a real kick out of it. The way he smiled at me ... Gosh.

"It's so good to see you, sweetie. I'd hug you, but I'm covered in potato peels and half a tub of sour cream." She stared down at the white splatters on her jacket. I opened my mouth to speak but she shook her head and cut me off. "Don't ask, cause I don't have an answer for you. I can't even remember touching the sour cream, much less spilling it."

Kent knocked his shoulder against mine. "She's a disaster in the kitchen." He'd said it loud enough for her to hear, and I half-expected her to pull him over her knee and give him a whooping in front of me, but she just snarled up her nose at him like a dog readying herself to attack. She let out a growl and everything.

"Watch it," she said, kicking her foot against the kitchen tiles like a bull preparing to lunge. I didn't know what the heck was going on and Kent didn't give me any time to find out.

"Watch this," Kent said before sticking his tongue out at his mother. He grabbed my wrist and yanked me out of the kitchen, then rushed us through the living room. As I held onto my overnight bag for dear life, Mrs. Fox let out a cackle behind us, and I figured she'd just gone back to peeling potatoes.

I was wrong.

As we took the stairs two at a time, she raced behind us. Kent dragged me through the small, second-floor hallway, to the last door on the right. He opened the door and shoved me through, following quickly behind. As he tried to close the door, she slammed through it and grabbed Kent, lifting him off his feet and giving him a big, bear hug.

"Oh my God, stop!" he yelled, laughing so hard tears were pooling in his eyes. She rubbed him back and forth against her shirt, smearing sour cream all over him. "I'm going to stink!"

After a few more rubs, she held him in her arms, hugging him tight. At first, I thought he might object and say she was embarrassing him in front of his company. I didn't like the idea of him thinking I was judging him for giving his mom affection. I wouldn't have. Me and Momma, we never really had that kind of relationship. She wasn't big on hugging. Daddy was, though. He was warmth and affection, through and through. Kent craned his neck, giving his mother a kiss on the cheek. She returned his kiss and set him back on the ground before turning toward me.

"Dinner should be done in a couple of hours. I'll call you both down when it's ready. If you need anything, you just let me know, alright sweetie?"

I nodded. "Yes, Mrs. Fox." Crap. I was supposed to call her Sister Fox. I called all the class supervisors at school Sister. When moms and dads came to get their kids from school, I'd call them Brother or Sister, too. I didn't know much about evangelical people aside from what I saw at school, and I didn't want to offend her. "Sorry! I didn't mean to call you 'Mrs.', Mrs. Fox." I closed my eyes and groaned. I'd been there less than five minutes and I'd already behaved like a fumbling, bumbling fool. "I didn't mean to say it that time, either, if it helps."

Mrs. Fox snorted. "Sweetheart, you can call me whatever you want, so long as you don't call me a pagan." She winked at me.

"A what?"

"A pagan," she repeated like it made a lick of sense to me. She frowned. "That was supposed to be a joke."

"It didn't land," Kent said flatly, and when she shot him a dirty look, he just stuck his tongue out, making her chuckle.

"Well, the point is, it doesn't bother me to be called 'Mrs. Fox' by someone who isn't part of the church. Now, if you ever decided to join, it would be a different story."

"I liked your church," I said. "I really liked the music."

"You did?" She had a hopeful look in her eyes, and I think she was hoping I'd ask about visiting again. I wanted to. Even with all the dancing and the crazy man running on the back of the pews, I loved the way it felt like there were stars humming with static in my chest whenever the music would swell. The way men held their hands to the sky, closed their eyes, and cried out their love for the Lord. The air itself felt alive.

"Would it be okay if I came back sometime?"

"We would love to have you, Grayson."

I shoved my hands in my pockets. "Thank you, Mrs. Fox."

Kent gave her a stern look that would have earned me pop on the butt if I'd given it to Momma. "Don't tell Dad, okay? Not tonight, at least. He'll start preaching and then we won't get to spend any time together."

Mrs. Fox nodded. "You're right. As much as I love a Joel Fox sermon, it's probably not the best form of entertainment for a sleepover. Why don't you boys just stay up here once dinner is over. Dad and I can spend the evening going over Sunday's sermon." She turned and arched an eyebrow at me. "Which I'll expect to see you at, young man."

"I'll be there," I agreed, excited to hear more of her singing. Mrs. Fox's voice was one of the prettiest I'd ever heard. Back home, our songs were drab and were usually sung off-key. I wasn't used to hearing someone who sounded like they belonged on the radio. "I can't wait."

When she was gone, Kent gave me the grand tour. Kent's bed was on the far wall, in line with the door. Over to the left, he had a small desk that was covered with books and a female bobblehead. She had red hair with blonde streaks in the front, and she was wearing a dress with a British flag on it. I wanted to ask about it, but he pulled me forward and shoved me down on his bed. He stared down at his pink flamingo shirt, now covered in sour cream, and laughed.

"I need to change," he said. He walked past his desk to his closet and pulled out a shirt. I stared down at my feet as he peeled off the sour cream flamingo. He was turned away from me, and I peeked up a few times, taking notice of his pale skin. He had freckles all across his shoulders, and I kind of wanted to trace them with my fingertips. I didn't have a reason for wanting to do it, but it seemed like it might be fun. He was a little chunky around the middle, but it suited him. Every time we hugged, it was like hugging the warmest, coziest pillow, and it always left me wanting more.

I thought I'd been sneaky enough with my stolen glances, but after he'd been standing shirtless a lot longer than it should have taken to change, I glanced up. His head was turned back, watching me as I watched him.

"Are you alright, Gray?"

I chewed my lower lip, stopping long enough to say, "Yeah" before pulling it back between my teeth. Kent slipped into a clean shirt and made his way back to the bed, plopping down right beside me.

I pointed at the small television and VCR in his room. "I thought you said your daddy only uses the television to watch his sermons. He lets you have one in your room, too?"

"He thinks I use it to watch old episodes of that Christian show, *The 700 Club*. Ms. Dottie from church pretends to tape them for me each week, but she really records movies off the Lifetime channel." He clapped his hands in front of his face, then slowly brought them down, twinkling his fingers like it was raining confetti. "So much drama!"

I snorted a laugh and leaned in, bumping my shoulder against his. chest. "You're the biggest drama queen I've ever met. I bet you'd fit right in.'

He lay on his back, spreading his arms like an angel when he landed. "True, though hardly the point.' Propping himself on his elbow, he gave me a nod, motioning for me to join him, lying back and turning my head in his direction.

We lay on his bed for half an hour, talking about the other kids at school. Eventually, he said we ought to do something fun. He leaned over the side of the bed and reached between his mattress and box springs, fishing around for some item he'd hidden away. With the way he was bent over in front of me, it put his entire butt on display.

I swallowed.

Gosh.

The room seemed about ten degrees hotter than it had been a few seconds before.

"Aha!" Kent shouted in victory. "Found it. Have you ever heard of the Spice …"

I didn't know why he stopped talking, but I really wished he hadn't. I liked it when he talked. Hearing that voice of his, all light and airy like he was a princess in a Disney movie. Tearing my eyes away from his backside, I looked up to find Kent staring right at me, his face pale and pasty, beads of sweat forming against his brow.

"Girls," he said.

I swallowed. "Girls?"

He pulled his arm from beneath the mattress, and he was holding a VHS tape. Part of me didn't want to look down and see what was on the cover. I thought it might be one of those dirty movies like the ones my brother kept hidden under the floorboard in his room. I didn't mind when Trevor would make me play lookout while he watched his movies, but I really didn't want Kent to ask me to do that. I hated having to listen from the other side of the door as Trevor watched men and women rolling around all sweaty and icky and putting things in weird places like they were playing naked Twister. He tried to make me watch one, once, but Momma knocked on the door a few seconds later. What I did manage to see made me feel queasy

Kent's big brown eyes were on full display, and normally they'd lock me in place, paralyzing me like that snake lady in the movie with Harry Hamlin I saw a few months before we moved to Texas. But now? Now my eyes were drifting back down to his ...

"What girls?" I blurted.

Kent grinned at me. A big one, just like his big butt. A smile that screamed genuine. It seemed like he knew what I'd been staring at and why I was staring at it. The recognition put me at ease. If he knew what all these new feelings were about, maybe he could clue me in, because I was at a loss.

When he rolled toward me, hiding his butt again, a sudden rush of disappointment that swept over me. Little waves of longing that that gathered at my ankles the way the water wrapped around them on the shore of the lake I found on our property a few weeks back.

I wondered if Kent would like the lake. Maybe we could go out there together and spend the day splashing each other and lounging in the sun next to the old oak tree by the water. It was probably more of a pond than a lake, but that wasn't the point—not when Kent's eyes were still burning holes in me. Gosh, why was he still looking at me like that? He was smiling like he did whenever I'd give him my Pringles at lunch.

He held out the tape; eyelashes fluttering adorably like he was putting on a show. I wanted to watch every single second of it. I wanted him to keep batting those pretty eyelashes and smiling bashfully, playing over and over on an endless loop.

"Hey," I whispered. "Hey, Kent. Fancy seeing you here." The second the words were out, I groaned, covering my face with my hand. His fingers curled around my wrist, sending pins and needles racing all over. I lowered my hand, but he didn't let go.

"Hey, Gray." His voice was soft and sweet, just like him. "Fancy seeing you here, too." He held the tape out for me. When I took it and stared at the cover, my heart sank. There were five women wearing loudly colored outfits that left little to the imagination. The word "Spice" was scrawled across the top.

Dang it. It really was a dirty movie. Why did it hurt to know Kent had a dirty movie with girls on the cover?

I didn't care how much Kent wanted to watch a bunch of girls rubbing all over each other; it wasn't happening with me in the room. Kent reached for the remote on his bedside table, our chests touching for the briefest moment. As he pulled back, he paused in front of me, our bodies making direct contact again.

"Showtime," he whispered. Leaving me in a breathless heap, he quickly whirled around, aimed the remote at the television, and turned it on. He sat up and held his hand out for me, and for a moment, I thought he was wanting to hold hands, but then he twitched his fingers, motioning for me to hand over the VHS.

It was too much. Too many feelings I didn't understand. Mostly anger because of that dang movie. I didn't want him to watch those men and women. I didn't want him to look at anyone like that. Wanting it gone, I threw the tape across the room, regretting it instantly.

Kent stared at me like I'd just slapped him, the sense of betrayal clear in his eyes. "Why'd you have to go and do that?"

"I don't want to watch a dirty movie, Kent. Why do you even have that? How the heck did you get it? Your daddy's a pastor, for Pete's sake."

"Dirty movie?" His eyes widened as he stared at me, and then, the loudest laugh I'd ever heard. He laughed until he was snorting, and then he doubled over, his arms wrapped around his stomach. Hearing him laugh at me hurt. I'd been used to bullies back in Little Rock, but nothing Kent had ever said gave me any indication he might be one, too. My eyes got a little misty, and when he noticed, the smile and laughter faded.

"What's wrong?" he asked.

You, I wanted to say. *You're supposed to be my friend, and I ain't ever had one before, so stop ruining it!*

"I wanna go home." I hopped off his bed and walked to the dresser, grabbing my overnight bag and slinging it over my shoulder. I was halfway to the door when Kent grabbed me by the wrist and spun me around.

"It's not a dirty movie. It's a concert. I thought you'd like it. They're my favorite band." He blushed. "I don't watch it because I think they're pretty or anything. I just really love their music. But I've never told that to anyone else, they'd just laugh at me." The look of disappointment on his face looked just as hurt as I felt when I first saw the tape, and it made me feel like a monster for putting it there. "I thought you were going to be different from the rest of them."

He was sad. He was sad, and it was because of me. I didn't care for that one bit. Kent wanted to share a hidden part of himself with me, and I took that part and threw it across the room. I dropped my bag on the floor and grabbed his tape, thankful to see it still intact.

"I'm sorry. Trevor watches those dirty movies sometimes and I thought ..." I sighed, shoving my hands inside my pockets and digging my fingernails into the fabric against my thighs. "I don't like them."

I was staring at my feet, too embarrassed to look up. Kent put his finger under my chin and tilted my face up until we were eye to eye. "I don't like those movies either. Tommy tried to give me a magazine with a bunch of naked women in it once. I told Sister Thorpe and he got suspended for a month. He had to come to the altar and confess that Sunday. I'm pretty sure he wanted to beat me up. He probably still does."

"If he ever touches you, I'll knock his lights out," I promised. "You can count on that."

"Yeah?" I handed him the cassette, wishing he'd taken my hand instead.

Gosh, what in the heck was going on with me?

"Can we watch it?" I asked.

"You want to?"

"It's important to you. If it's important to you, it's important to me."

His face lit up like the Fourth of July. "Thanks, Gray."

I took a seat at the foot of his bed as he walked to the TV sitting on his dresser and popped the tape into the VCR. When he made his way back, I figured he'd want to sit on the other end of the bed, but he plopped down right next to me. Our knees knocked, and he turned to me and flashed a grin.

"It's okay if you don't like it. We don't have to watch them if you—"

I grabbed his hand and squeezed. "We'll watch it. Start to finish."

When he hit play, five women stood in the center of a stage. The women were wearing more of those really colorful outfits. As they sang about spicing up their lives, I darted my eyes down at him, trying to be inconspicuous. He was kind of bopping along to the music, and with his hands at his sides, he was moving stealthily following along with their dance steps. When the redhead flung her hand forward, pointing at the crowd, Kent moved his arm slightly. As the lady with the ponytail rolled her hips around in a circle, he followed along, but on a much smaller scale, making the bed shake.

He was dancing.

Kent Fox was dancing with them, and he knew every move. His face was still as a stone, like he was hiding away his happiness because he was scared it might peek through. I wanted him to. He deserved to shine. More than anything, I wanted to see him dance. To see him lose himself in excitement. His hand rested on the mattress, forefinger pointing out alongside one of the women. She had big, curly hair, just like his. I realized I still had his other hand in mine, and I didn't want to let it go.

"You know the moves?" I asked. He winced, like he thought I was making fun of him. I would never. "Will you teach me?"

His jaw went slack, mouth gaping. "Really?"

"Yeah. Yeah, Kent. Show me."

He stood up, his hand squeezing mine, as he pulled me along for the ride. He hit pause and stared at me. "You promise you won't laugh?"

"We're friends. Friends don't make fun of each other. You don't have to worry about that with me. Not now, and not ever."

His smile spread again, and he gave me a nod. Turning back toward the TV, he stared at the women on screen. Ruffling his shoulder like a peacock, he said, "Okay, so when they get to the chorus—that's the part where Scary Spice starts talking about people of the world—"

"Scary?"

"Yeah, the one with the curly hair."

"She doesn't look very scary to me."

Kent rolled his eyes. "No, that's her Spice name. Scary Spice. My favorite is Ginger, though. Which one's yours?"

I stared at the women paused on the screen. Was he asking me which one I thought was prettiest? Because the longer I looked, the more confused I got. Trevor was always talking about which girls he thought were pretty, and all the creepy, nasty things he'd like to do with them. Stuff with private parts and mouths and tongues. I tried to picture myself doing those things with girls, but I felt nothing. Turning back to Kent, a picture popped into my head. Kent and me. Kent and me hugging. Kent and me kissing each other on the cheek. *Kent-Kent-Kent.*

"The blonde one!" I said with too much force.

He smirked. "*Baby.*"

I whimpered. Why the heck did I whimper?

"Huh?"

"Baby Spice. That's Emma."

"Oh," I said, not sure where the disappointment had come from.

"Anyway ..." He shoved his mound of curls over his head and to the side, exposing that pale, creamy-skinned neck of his. It was redder than usual, and I wasn't sure if it was down to the room's temperature, or if he was feeling all of those strange feelings I'd been feeling, too.

"Alright. Just follow along." Kent closed his eyes, tilting his neck until it cracked. He was a dramatic stick of dynamite, his every movement drawn out with sizzling explosions, leaving the air around him smelling of sulfur and sass.

"Slam it to the left," he sang, slamming his arm down at his side. "To the right," his hip popped out to the right, arm following alongside the women on the screen. "To the front!" I snorted when Kent humped the air in front of him, pumping his hand forward like the lady with the ponytail. As the women swayed their arms in the air like they were doing the tango, Kent followed in their footsteps, his arm stretched high as he twirled his wrist. He grabbed the VCR remote and pressed pause.

"You got it?"

"I think so."

"Good. Okay, Collins. Let's do this." He hit play, and we danced. Gosh, we danced.

After an hour of Kent teaching me choreography, he put the tape back in its case and slid it under his mattress, telling me his daddy wouldn't approve of it, but his momma didn't mind.

"We should take our showers now so we don't have to waste time after dinner," Kent said. For reasons I didn't understand, he leaned closer and sniffed under my arm, looking up through his lashes. "You're smelling pretty funky." I gaped at him, but he just tossed a wink at me. "I didn't say I didn't like it. Come on, I'll show you where the bathroom is. You can go first, then I'll take one."

He led me to the bathroom, carrying my overnight bag with him. He unzipped my bag and started digging through my things. At first, I wanted to object, but then he pulled out a pair of my underwear, his eyes darting back and forth at my waist and at them.

"Dang, Gray. I didn't take you for a boxer-briefs kind of guy."

I grabbed them out of his hand and held them behind my back, but I couldn't hide the smile spreading across my face. I gave him a shrug, because I couldn't think of anything else to do. He kept going through my bag, pulling out my night shirt and sleep shorts. His fingers traced Tommy Pickles from Rugrats' face and beamed at the fabric.

I blushed, worried he'd ask me what a teenager was doing watching a baby show, but he just turned to me and held them out to me.

"Ms. Dottie records *Rugrats* for me every now and then. I've always been a fan of Anjelica, myself."

"But she's a bully."

"I love a good villain," he said with a smirk. "Can I tell you a secret?"

"Tell me," I insisted, grabbing the shorts, my finger tingling when it touched his palm.

"I like to root for the bad guys when I watch television. It drives Mom crazy. She says she sometimes thinks I'm filled with the devil."

"Are you?" I didn't know if it even mattered at that point. I had a friend. A real friend who didn't care that I wore little kid pajamas or that I danced like a fool. He could worship that Lisa Rinna lady from that soap opera Momma watched, for all I cared.

"You're just going to have to hang around long enough to find out, aren't you?" Kent turned toward the bathtub and twisted the tap, holding his hand under the faucet until the water was warm enough for his liking.

Was he going to shower with me? Is that what was happening? I hadn't had a friend in a long time, but I didn't remember shared showers being a thing. While I worried, I stared at the back of his shorts. They clung to him like a second skin, and I took in the sight of him. I enjoyed the stitching. The outline of the pockets across his butt. A peculiar thing to notice, but that's what I'd done. Noticed it. Focused on it. Stared at it like it was going out of style.

He looked over his shoulder at me and stared, I lifted my eyes until they met his, and I gave him a smile. There was something in his gaze I couldn't make out. Something hidden in plain sight, but the message lost on me. He flashed me another smile before walking past me. Stopping at the door, he pointed at the cabinet hanging over the toilet.

"The towels are in there if you need one."

I arched an eyebrow at him. Of course, I would need one. Did he think I was just going to drip dry for the rest of the night? I chuckled to myself before walking to the door and shoving him outside.

"Don't take too long," he said, scrunching up his nose. "I miss you already." Kent stuck his tongue out at me as he jerked the door shut behind him. I reached for the knob, meaning to lock it, only to find there wasn't one. A rush of panic flooded my veins, because locks were a must at home. Trevor never met an unlocked door he didn't open. I'd made the mistake only a handful of times, usually when I was peeing, only to jump and spray urine all over the toilet. I definitely didn't want to pee all over Mrs. Fox's toilet.

"There's no lock," I shouted, hoping Kent was still on the other side.

The door cracked open, and Kent wedged his face between the door and the frame. "Don't need one. No one will bother you."

I stared down at my feet. "You're sure?"

Kent's cool hand against my face took me by surprise. I jerked my head in his direction, my eyes widening. "Promise." He drew his thumb and forefinger together, pinching my cheek. "No one's going to sneak a peek at your privates. Not on my watch, buddy." He gave me another nod, and then he was gone, the door crashing closed behind him.

Kent had so many neat things in his shower. There was a yellow rubber duck that looked just as old as Kent, and a blue loofa that he probably used every day. It was hanging on a rope around the showerhead, just begging to be touched. I brought the loofah to my face, taking a quick sniff. I didn't have a reason for doing it, it just felt like the right thing to do. Then I realized Kent used it day after day, shower after shower, rubbing it all over. His chest. Arm. Legs. *Everywhere.* Even down there.

I took another sniff before hanging back where I found it and finishing up my shower.

Once I was dressed, I opened the door and found him sitting against the wall opposite me. He had a book in his hand, giving it his undivided attention. I cleared my throat to alert him that I was done.

"Feel better?" he said, looking up at me.

I nodded. "So much better. Gosh, you've got a neat bathroom. Your soap is liquid!"

He snorted. "Yeah. Mom used to get the bars, but then I reminded her that I wash my nuts and my butt with it, and asked her how in the world that was sanitary."

I cringed, because his logic both made sense and made me sick. The words also sent a rush of heat through my body. I kind of wanted to find that bar of soap of his and hide it in my bag so I could take it home with me.

"Exactly," he said, standing up and walking past me into the bathroom. He pulled his shirt off, his eyes locked on mine for some reason. I looked down, taking in the sight of his shirtless chest. We looked alike for the most part; him a little thicker around the middle, but just as pale and pasty. There was no hair on his chest, just like me. He had a little under his arms which made me kind of jealous, but Daddy was a hairy man, so I knew it would come in time. A late bloomer; I think that's what he called me. Kent's eyes stayed on me as he pushed his pants down, and then he stood in just his underwear.

"You can either head back to my room or you can stay and we can make things awkward," he said with a giggle.

I spun around on my heels, but I didn't leave. I still wanted to ask him what that look was about.

His arm draped over my shoulder, his underwear dangling from his hand like a flag. "Do you mind throwing these in my hamper?"

I grabbed them without thinking. How could I think of anything aside from the fact that Kent Fox was completely naked behind me. And I was touching something that had just touched his ...

I closed my grip tighter, my eyes bulging at the realization.

"Okay!" I ran forward, leaving the door wide open in my wake. Kent laughed, but I didn't stick around to ask why.

In his room, I paused, staring at the underwear. I knew I shouldn't. I knew it was nasty and gross and probably made me a horrible person, but I lifted his underwear to face and breathed him in.

Kent.

It smelled just like him. Sweet and fruity. Maybe a little musky with the sweat from our dancing, but I didn't mind. I didn't mind one bit. After a few more deep breaths, I came to my senses and threw his dirty underwear in the hamper, then tried to clean up a little. We'd made a mess during our danceathon, especially when he insisted on costume changes. His clothes covered the floor, and I picked up the pieces up one by one, putting them back on their hangers and into his closet.

Once I was done with the clothes, I picked up our glasses of water, both still completely full, and walked toward the door. It flung open before I got to it, and I screeched from surprise.

Kent was standing in the doorway in nothing but a towel, and he was dripping wet. And then, so was I, because his sudden reappearance had scared me so badly, I threw my hands in the air, drenching myself in tap water and regret. Kent snorted and held his hand over his mouth, trying to not laugh. He came toward me, wrapping an arm around my shoulder and pulling me in for a hug.

"God, I like you, Gray." He brought his hand to the top of my head and rubbed his knuckles against my scalp playfully. His skin on mine felt impossible, because Kent Fox was nearly naked, and he was holding me in a way no one had held me before. When he eventually broke the hug, he stared down at my shorts and frowned. "Bummer. I was looking forward to hanging out with Tommy Pickles."

He winked at me.

I scowled at him.

He rolled his eyes and walked to his dresser, pulling out another shirt and a pair of shorts. "Are your underwear soaked, too?"

"Y-yeah," I stuttered.

Kent dug through the dresser for a few seconds before pulling out a pair of bright blue boxer-briefs and tossing them over his shoulder. "Will these work?"

They were cute. Even better, Kent had worn them before. His most intimate article of clothing was about to be shielding my privates, cupping them and holding on tight. It was a realization that made my stomach spin. After setting the underwear on his bed and laying the shirt and shorts beside them, I peeked over my shoulder to make sure he wasn't staring. His eyes were focused ahead as he pulled out a blue shirt with a crucifix on the front. He sighed and mumbled something under his breath.

Once my shirt was off, I slid my shorts down, feeling exposed standing behind him in nothing but my skivvies. I nervously glanced over my shoulder again and was greeted with Kent's naked butt. I swallowed, because the sight of it was doing something to me on the inside. I'd never felt it before, but it was warm and it was fuzzy, and I didn't particularly dislike the sensation.

I shoved my thumbs under my wet boxer-briefs and shoved them down, just trying to get it over with before Kent turned around. I reached for the boxers he'd handed to me, fumbling nervously with the underwear, trying to pull them up in my rush to cover my bare butt. I must have been moving a little too quickly, because I tripped on my ankle and fell onto the floor. Kent whirled around on his heel and opened his mouth to speak, stopping when he saw the naked boy lying on his floor.

He stared at me.

I stared right back.

"Dang," Kent said with a strange look in his eyes. An intense heat ran across the sides of my face. Kent was staring at my ...

I shielded myself with my hands, feeling mortified. I watched his face, seeking out his reaction. Would he laugh? Would he make fun of me?

He was staring at me the same way he would stare when I'd bring a helping of Momma's blackberry cobbler to school for him. He licked his lips, color spreading across his cheeks.

When he laughed, it wasn't mean or cruel like I'd expected. It was full of affection. We stood there, neither of us speaking for an uncomfortable length of time. Finally, he arched an eyebrow in my direction and smirked.

"I didn't realize my best friend was walking around with a two-liter bottle between his legs."

Gosh.

Kent was holding onto his package, hiding it with his hand, but that hand fell away, leaving me with an unobstructed view of his manhood.

Oh-gosh, oh-gosh, oh-my-freaking-gosh.
There he is.

I panted, my breathing harsh and fast. When I looked at him, I was looking at him the same way Trevor looked at the girlfriends he would bring to the house for Sunday supper. The way Daddy used to look at Momma before we moved to Texas.

Kent slid his foot into the leg of his underwear, then the other, and he pulled them up, snapping the elastic band against his hips. When he was done, he crossed his arms over his chest and smiled down at me.

It was like he was silently accusing me. I needed to change the subject. To lead us out of the confusion I'd hurled us into. Kent's penis wasn't much smaller than mine, but I figured I could make light of the situation.

"Two liter, huh?" I forced a smile that did nothing to alleviate the nerves running around inside of me like headless chickens. "If you want, I can see if there's some kind of operation they can do to lend you a little bit of mine. It might help with the fact that you've only got a half a pint under those." I pointed at his underwear.

Kent scrunched up his nose and glared like he wanted to smack me. "Oh, you're in for it now," he said before launching himself toward the ground and landing directly on top of me. We tumbled around on the floor, taking turns pinning each other down. I'd never been a fan of wrestling, but wrestling with Kent wasn't nearly as boring as the WWE matches Trevor and Daddy would watch at night. Arms and legs and bare skin enveloped me. We came to a standstill when he wound up on top of me, pinning me to the ground by my shoulders.

"Take it back," he demanded, trying to keep a straight face.

I shook my head and tried to shift my shoulders to break loose, but his hold was too tight. "Never!"

"Take it back, Grayson!" He pulled one hand back, and I knew that was my chance, but before I could launch him off of me, he wedged his hand into my armpit and tickled me. I let out a cackle, wriggling and writhing on the floor.

"I've got a big one, too. Say it!" His fingers dug deeper, and he brought his right hand to my hip, tickling up and down my side.

"Stop! Oh my gosh, Kent, stop it!"

His hands went still, he winked at me, and then he beat on his chest with his fists, reared back his head, and shouted, "Never!" like I had moments before.

My skin was a little colder when he took his hands away. So when he brought them back to my sides, I didn't even really mind the tickling, just as long as it meant I got to be a little closer to him.

"Come on, *Two-liter*," he said with a smirk. "Say it."

"Okay—okay—okay," I managed. "Just stop and I will!"

He stopped tickling me, his hands resting on my sides. "Say it," he whispered.

I nodded, trying to keep my face as serious as possible. "Kent Fox ..."

"Yes?"

"Has got ..." I rose up until the tips of our noses touched. "The smallest thing I've ever seen!"

He roared like a lion, and then his hands were digging—scraping—tickling my sides. "I hate you, Gray Collins. I hate everything about you." It went on for another minute or so before he collapsed beside me. We laid there, neither of us speaking as we tried to catch our breath. I turned my head to the side and stared at him. After a minute or so, he caught sight of me and mirrored my pose, head to the side, eyes locked on mine. He held his arm out at his side, wedging it behind my head so I could use him like a pillow. I laid against him, enjoying the way his warm skin felt against my cool neck. I turned on my side, burrowing my face against his chest. He laughed, soft and light, but it was there. Guiding me. Leading me to the promised land. His chest was soft, like a warm cotton sheet fresh from the dryer.

"Can I tell you a secret?" he whispered.

"You can tell me anything, *Half-pint*." I liked the way the nickname felt as it fell off my tongue. Quirky. Sassy. *Cute.*

Just like Kent.

Oh, my Gosh. Kent Fox is cute.

"I didn't have this before you moved here." He closed his eyes as if he was ashamed of the words. I wanted to shake him by the shoulders and tell him he didn't have to be ashamed. That there was no embarrassment when it came to us. Not then. Not ever. "A friend, I mean. A real one. The kids at school picked on me a lot. I was lonely a lot."

"Well, now you do," I whispered. "Now you've got a best friend, and you ain't ever got to be lonely again."

Chapter Four

June 2001

"For God's sake, Two-liter, would you come on already?"

Kent was in one of his sassy, over-the-top moods. The ones where it felt like he was ready to rip the whole world in two with the might of his voice.

We'd been in the garage for half an hour, searching for a lighter. I didn't know what the heck we needed a lighter for, but he'd said it was "simply a must" as he held the back of his hand against his forehead like a dainty little thing, so I relented. If Kent wanted a lighter, Kent would get a lighter. We tore through toolboxes and upended his dad's entire workbench. After an almost-endless search, Kent finally shouted, "I found one!"

I turned around to see him holding a white lighter. Kent took a step toward me, and I took a step back. Then another. And another, until I was pressed against the garage door. I didn't know where his aunt had run off to. All I knew was Kent Fox was staring at me with a look I hadn't seen before. Head tilted. Lips curling. Nostrils flaring. Breaths coming out hot and heavy. He approached slowly, his eyes traveling up and down my body. We didn't speak, both of us lost in whatever this moment between us was. In my entire life, I'd never been as scared as I was right then.

There was something in his hand; small and round, like one of those long, skinny cigarettes we'd catch Sister Fox smoking when she thought we were upstairs sleeping. We'd caught her more than enough times in the last three years for me to familiarize myself with their shape. Kent held it in the air, wiggled his eyebrows at me, and he ran his tongue across his lips, wetting them.

Wetting them for me?

God Almighty, was this it?

"What do you say, Gray ... Puff-puff-pass?"

If it hadn't been for my eyelids, I was pretty sure my eyes might have bulged out of my head entirely. It was one those marijuana cigarettes Sister Thorpe warned us about at school. A gatekeeper's drug, I think she called it. She also mentioned something about peer pressure, which was when a friend tried to talk you into making terrible life choices. I could hear my mother's voice in my head so clearly, it almost sounded like she was right beside us.

If Kent asked you to jump off a bridge, would you?

I was ashamed to admit I would. I trusted him with my life. With my heart. With my eternal soul. If what I felt for him was really as wrong as Kent's daddy preached every Sunday at West Clark Apostolic Chapel—if my soul was already damned—there was no one I'd rather burn alongside.

"Aunt Jeanie slipped this into my pocket before she went to bed." He licked his lips, leaving them glistening against the harsh, overhead lighting. "Do you trust me?"

"Kent," I said, shaking my head. "We can't."

He smiled as he brought it to his lips. "It's just a joint, Two-liter. Nothing to be scared of."

"You've done it before? Taken ..." I peeked around the garage, weary of nonexistent watchful eyes. "You've taken marijuana?"

Kent snorted, leaning his head forward, pressing it against my chest, and letting out a deep, guttural laugh that built up in his belly and poured out like a volcano. "You're adorable sometimes." Reaching up, he squeezed the tip of my nose gently. "I can't wait to see how much more adorable you get when you're high."

I swallowed. "It's illegal, though."

He rolled his eyes and took a few steps back. "For God's sake, Two-liter, we're sixteen. It's not like we're shooting up heroin. It's just a little pot. Fucking chill, dude."

"I really wish you wouldn't talk like that. You know it makes me nervous."

He put the joint in his mouth and flicked the lighter. The smell was strong, like a dead skunk on the side of the road. He inhaled, breathing in a lungful of smoke. Tilting his head to the ceiling, he closed his eyes. His face was bathed in harsh overhead lighting, but it didn't matter what sort of light was touching Kent's face, because he would be beautiful no matter what. After a few seconds, his smile widened and smoke pushed out through the small crags between his teeth.

"Does it hurt?" I asked, tapping my chest. "Does it burn or something?"

He nodded, his mouth forming an O as the last of the smoke escaped him. "Not too bad. The first time I did it, it felt like I was going to hack up a lung."

"And that's what you want me to do? Set my dang lungs on fire?"

He stared at me with an intense look I couldn't really read. "I want you to feel good, Grayson." Kent held the joint out for me. I wanted to grab it, but something was holding me back. Noticing my unease with the situation, he smiled encouragingly at me. "You don't have to be scared. It feels really good."

I shrugged. It was all brand new to me. Even when Trevor and his friends brought home that bottle of wine Kyle nicked from his parents' liquor cabinet, I hadn't been able to push past my own fear long enough to take a swig. I'd wanted to. They acted giggly and silly, and I wanted to join them in that headspace. Then I got scared. Scared of Momma and Daddy, but mostly scared of what God might think.

Kent walked toward me and put his hand on my shoulder, giving it a squeeze. "I'd never do something that was going to hurt you. It'll feel good, Two-liter. Let me make you feel good."

Gosh, I wanted that. I wanted his hands everywhere. Wanted his lips all over. But that wasn't the good time he was offering me, no matter how much I wanted it to be.

"I've got an idea," he said. "It'll make it easier for you. Jeanie did this with me last time she was here. She called it a shotgun."

He put the end with the fire inside his mouth, closing his lips around it. His hand cupped the side of my face, gently brushing his thumb back and forth against my cheek. When he approached, it felt like tiny little firecrackers booming to life inside of me.

His lips.

They were coming right at me.

I opened my mouth and closed my eyes, just wanting to soak in the moment. When the end of the joint was in my mouth, he breathed in through the hot end, sending smoke misting over my tongue. Kent had said it would be easier if I just breathed in and reminded myself it was all okay. I tried to do that, but it was hard when his hand was rubbing my cheek like that.

He was giving me deep, endless eye contact that tore through my defenses, leaving me still as stone. His lips were less than an inch away, but one inch between us was still one too many, so I moved closer until we touched. Kent held the joint between his teeth, but I could see the panic in his eyes. He was about two seconds away from losing his marbles, so I moved closer one last time, then I pulled away. When we separated, he stared at me, eyes narrowed, nostrils flaring, he pulled the joint out of his mouth and bent down, putting it out against the concrete flooring. Then he smiled at me. Standing upright, he moved on me like a shadow. We were inches apart, and still, he moved closer.

That smile. It was overpowering, and seeing him coming closer—watching the distance disappear between him and I—I freaked. I feigned a cough, choking on air like I was hacking up a lung. Kent went into protector mode, stroking my back as he tried to comfort me.

"I'm fine."

"I'm sorry. Did I give you too much?"

"It's okay," I said, trying not to gag at the nasty smell of Kent's joint. As I took a step back, my head went heavy. It was like the edges of my eyes were fuzzy, and my face felt like a pillow. I wondered if Kent wanted to lie on it.

"You can put your head on me if you want," I blurted.

"What?"

"My face," I said, grabbing his hand and pressing it against my cheek. "It's soft and warm. Probably fuzzy, too. You can sleep on me all night, Kent. I don't mind. Honest." Kent arched an eyebrow at me. "Or you can give me another one of those handguns."

"Shotguns, Grayson. They're called shotguns."

"Whatever. Any gun. Whatever gun you want to give me, I'll take it. It was fun, wasn't it? When you were blowing me, I mean."

Kent started choking, banging the side of his fist against his chest as he doubled over and held himself up with his hand on his knee. "Jesus Christ." He slammed his fist against his chest a few more times before standing upright. "Blowing you?"

"The smoke," I said with a nod. I didn't know why the heck he almost choked to death, but I'd have to remember to ask him in the morning. "When you blew it in my mouth. Then our lips touched and it was almost like we were …"

His eyes widened again, and he took a step back.

Crap.

"Almost like we were what?"

I chewed on my lip just to keep my big mouth shut.

"Gray?"

"Like we were singing," I attempted. "Your song. Just for you, Half-pint. Remember?"

His body relaxed a little, but I could tell he wasn't buying what I was trying to sell him. "I remember." He pulled the lighter from his pocket and brought the joint back to his lips, sucking, pulling fire through the herb, the tip glowing bright and orange. He pulled in a mouthful, holding it in his lungs as he tried to speak through the smoke. "Just for me."

I wanted to bring a smile to that frightened face. To make him light up like he always did when I sang it to him. I took a step toward him, and then another. He exhaled, the strong stench of skunk and rot wafting directly toward me. I leaned forward, my mouth hanging open, and I bit at the smoke. Sucked it in and held.

His air. Kent's air was in my mouth, giving me sustenance. I pressed my finger to his lip, motioning for him to open them, but he just kissed my fingertip.

I rolled my eyes, because I wasn't trying to give him a cheap thrill. I wanted to give his air back to him. Pulling my finger down, his bottom lip tugged, and when I let go, it bounced up and down like a slinky. Tapping the side of his jaw, I waited. Finally, he got the hint and opened his mouth. I leaned forward, pressing my lips to his, and I blew.

My exhale ended on a whimper, and more than anything, I wanted to run my fingers through his hair. To tug on those curls until I made him moan. To spear his mouth with my tongue until all that existed in this world were our connected lips and our dueling tongues.

He wrapped his arms around my waist and pulled me closer, the lump in his pants pressing against mine. His hands dug into my ribs, and then he tickled me, heavy and harsh. I cackled into his face, and when the giggles overtook him, he laughed so hard that he hacked, blasting the smoke against my face. His tickle torture continued, and I couldn't handle it any more. I pressed my arms against his chest and tried to push him off of me.

"Let go, Kent," I said, trying to wriggle away from him.

Kent snorted, and then he coughed, sending spittle spattering against my cheek. He looked deep into my eyes, the corner of his lip curling up. He had such pretty lips. Pink and pillowy and begging to be sucked. I'd pictured them so many times—usually imagining how they would look wrapped around my ...

"You've got really pretty lips," I whispered.

Kent's entire body went rigid. His hands fell to his sides, and he took a step back. I couldn't read the look in his eyes. Couldn't make sense of the fire flashing in them. Those big browns I loved so much were harsh. Harsher than I'd ever seen them.

"I think Kyle's gay," he said.

What? What the heck did that have to do with anything? "Huh?"

"I'm pretty sure he was flirting with me at lunch the other day." He stared at me as if he was trying to read something written on my forehead. If Kyle was flirting with Kent, I'd deck him right in the face. Kent was mine. Mine, mine, mine.

"That's disgusting," were the only words I could think of. "He's got another thing coming if he thinks he's touching you. I'll punch his face in. You tell him to keep his creepy hands off you"

Kent winced like I'd somehow hurt him. I might have been high, but I knew Kent. I should have been able to read his expression, but at that moment, I couldn't.

"I mean it, Kent. Tell him to keep his gosh-dang hands off of you. It's sick." Sick of Kyle to think he could touch what was mine. Sick of him for thinking I'd let him touch all over Half-Pint's body when even I hadn't had the chance to touch him yet. I took a step forward, and Kent took a step back, banging his head on the back of his Daddy's tool cabinet. "Don't worry, I'll kick his butt if he does it again. You just tell me and I'll take care of it, okay?"

Kent sighed, his eyes focusing on our feet. "Yeah, Gray. Yeah, I'll tell you."

Good. Kent was mine. He knew he was mine, and I was his. The way we'd always been. And what right did Kyle have coming in trying to shake that up? We were Two-liter and Half-pint. There was no room for another cup, quart, or gallon. Not even a dang teaspoon.

I grabbed his hand and tugged, leading him out of the garage and onto the driveway. Honey Lane had never been a hotbed of happenings. Kent's house, and two other homes shared the cul-de-sac. The owners of those homes were in their nineties, and judging by the darkened windows in the distance, it was well past their bedtime. The Texas stars, big and bright, were shining down on us like our own personal spotlights. It felt like they were dancing above us. Like God had opened the sky up like a music box, and dazzling ballerinas twinkled to the tune of a familiar hymn.

Kent stood behind me, arms looping over my shoulders as he held me close against his chest. A familiar hymn hummed low within my soul, demanding release. He loved it when I sang to him, especially his special song—the one that had only ever been meant for him. What he didn't know was just how much that song meant to me, too. He didn't know it had always been my love letter to him. A quiet confession of who he was to me.

"*In life, in death, o Kent, abide with me,*" I sang, just for him.

"Grayson," he whispered into my ear. And then, "God, Gray."

"Just for you, Half-pint," I reminded him, holding his hands to my chest. "It's always been just for you." I wasn't really sure if I was still talking about the song, but I knew my words were facts. I felt the truth of them flowing through my blood like the Holy Ghost itself. "You know that, don't you?"

"Just for me," he said, his voice husky and light all at the same time.

I felt Him in that moment. God, coaxing me closer. He was calling out to me, wanting to talk. I wanted it just as much as He did. To take communion and bask in his light. He was too far away, though. I knew I needed to get closer. My head was humming, and my heart was on fire, but I heard God right there in that driveway.

I started going to Kent's church the Sunday following our first sleepover. I started off slowly, just going to Sunday service every week. Then Kent would ask if I wanted to go to his youth group meeting, or he'd invite me to the Saturday night potlucks. Eventually, I was going four times a week, and over time, the congregants became like a second family to me. Momma and Daddy still hadn't decided on a home church, but she'd come with me sometimes. She would always have her eyes locked on Kent and me, watching to see what we were getting up to during Pastor Fox's sermon.

Over the years I realized Pastor Fox was a hateful man with a hateful heart. I knew I needed to love him as my brother in Christ, but he made it really hard sometimes, always yelling and screaming about gays and Democrats, like they were the worst thing on Earth. I was one of those two, and I was pretty sure Kent was both. He'd always talk about politics with me, but none of it made much sense. The way his daddy talked, you'd think gay people had single handedly brought about the end times.

Despite the hate Pastor Fox preached at us, I never felt that from God. Pastor Fox always talked about how the Lord would speak to his loyal subjects. He'd go on and on about the fire he felt in his belly, and the way the hairs on the back of his neck stood up each time God spoke through him. The rest of the church would dance and holler and praise God endlessly, all experiencing burning bellies and tingling necks. Kent told me I should just pretend like he does, but that would be a lie, and the thought of lying about God made me want to back away from Kent so I didn't get struck by however many lightning bolts God might send his way.

I was finally feeling it. The tingles. The burning tummy. I felt it all, and whether it was down to the Spirit, or if it was just because of the pot, I wasn't really sure. All I knew was God was calling out to me, and I wanted to answer Him.

I turned around, searching for something. Some way to get closer to Him.

"The roof, my precious child," God or the marijuana said.

I turned around and stared at Half-pint. "Stay right there. I gotta go talk to God." I turned on my heel and walked around the side of the house. Kent trailed behind, calling my name. "Just give me a minute, Kent. He asked me to meet him on the roof. He called me his precious child and everything. It was nice. We had a moment."

Kent snorted, and then he grabbed my wrist, holding me in place. "You're not going on the damn roof."

I scoffed at him and covered his mouth with my palm. "Hush. He can hear you. I just told you He was talking to me. Gosh, you shouldn't be cussing at all, but you definitely shouldn't be doing it when the Spirit's at work. Just sit down right …" I examined my surroundings and smiled when I spotted the tree trunk beside their house. "Sit right there and wait for me, okay? I won't be long. He probably just wants to thank me for my service."

"To thank you for your service? Are you a marine now?"

"Hush," I scolded him. "You know I don't condone violence. Even if it is for God and Country. I don't want anyone getting hurt, Kent. It's sad."

He pinched my cheek and grinned. "God, you're precious."

"True," I said with a nod. "Very true, actually, because God just said so himself, but it's beside the point. Now, you just sit over there and stay adorable. I'll be back in a few."

Kent chuckled, and his hand remained locked on my wrist. "Come on, let's head inside and get ready for bed. I'll let you use the shower first."

It's like he wasn't listening to a word I was saying. God was seeking me out and Kent was trying to stand in the way. I didn't want to see Kent struck down for blasphemy, so I improvised. He wasn't going to budge, so I eyed the second story bathroom window and formed a plan. It was a great plan, really. One might go as far as calling it foolproof.

"Fine. I'll shower. But then we're crawling in your bed, and I'm going to sing you to sleep. Okay?"

He pulled me in for another hug and laughed softly into my ear. "Sounds perfect."

Five minutes later, Kent was in his bedroom, and I was standing in the shower. I pointed the shower head down at the drain so it wouldn't hit me as I made my escape, and then I turned on the tap. Kent's bathroom looked out over the garage, and there was a slant that led up to the roof, so I knew as long as I could make it through the window, I could get up there and meet God himself.

It wasn't too difficult of a climb. Once I was out the window, I tiptoed across the top of the garage until I reached the slope leading to the top. It took me a few minutes to climb, but once I was there, I stood on the small patch of evened-out shingles.

My pants were snug. Too tight around my hips. Too tight against my thighs. My calves. Even my ankles. I had no explanation for my actions, other than I was high, and my pants didn't seem to fit anymore. I unbuttoned my jeans and sat on the roof before attempting to shake them off.

With my legs dangling over the edge, I shuffled the jeans off, sending them falling to the ground below. I peered over and took in a deep breath, because I didn't realize how high up the roof was.

It was like God was right above me. Constellations in the tapestry of sky, forming the face of the Almighty. I lifted my hand to the sky and offered him a wave. My head felt fuzzy and I was seeing God in the stars. A wave seemed appropriate for the occasion.

"Hey God, how's it hanging? Can I tell you a secret? I don't know that it's really a secret. You probably already know." I lay back against the shingles and stared up at God and the stars. "I'm gay," I whispered. I knew He could hear me, because the Bible says He hears all. Kent was in his room, and there was no way he could hear me up there, but the thought of him hearing those words had my hands shaking. I lowered my voice just in case. "I know Pastor Fox says it's a sin—that we're all just deviants—but I think you know better. I think you know better than all of us. When we came to West Clark, I didn't think I'd find a friend. I never had any back home ... but I found him because of you, didn't I? You knew I'd been lonely for a really long time, so you sent him to me. Or me to him." I shrugged, unable to hold back a giggle. Sitting back up, I beamed at him again. "Either way, you knew we needed each other; however you want to frame it. Thank you, God. Thank you for Kent."

Two arms wrapped around me from behind, hugging me around my waist.

"Thanks, God," Kent said as he pulled me against his chest. I peered up to find him staring down at me.

"Hey, Half-pint."

He leaned down and pressed a kiss to my forehead. "Hey, Gray." Kent looked around us, taking in the sight of the red shingles. "You're on the roof."

"I'm on the roof," I agreed. I pointed to the left and scowled. "Just watch out for that big glob of bird poop. I almost stepped in it earlier."

He chuckled. "Noted."

I smiled, because Kent had his arms around me. How the heck could I feel him pressed up against me like that and not? The stars were scorching throughout the sky, but he burned brighter than them all. His hands moved. Not much, just his fingertips grazing over my shirt, exploring my chest. I closed my eyes and bit back a moan.

"Are you okay?"

I looked up at him. "Yeah, I'm good. I'm always good when I'm with you."

"I'm always good when I'm with you, too." His fingertips tickled my stomach. "Why'd you climb out the window? I was worried."

I shrugged, staring up at the sky. "God's right there," I said, pointing at the biggest, brightest star in the sky. "He says, 'hi.'"

Kent laughed until he snorted, tilting his head and giving our Lord and savior a salute. "Howdy."

I pinched his thigh. "Kent?"

There was a warm, wet sensation against my nape that sent chills down my spine. I gripped his hand tighter, scared to say much more for fear of scaring him. His hips pushed forward, and his crotch was pressed up against my butt.

"You took off your pants," he said.

"They felt too tight." I turned back to stare at him. I didn't want to go back down yet. God and Kent's love were pouring through me, and I never wanted the moment to end. "Stay with me? Just a little while longer. Please?"

He took his coat off and laid it over my lap, covering my bare thighs. "You must be freezing, Two-liter." I grabbed his arm and pulled him against me, just needing to feel him closer.

"Then cuddle up close and keep me warm." I tickled his chin. "Do you ever wonder what we're gonna do when school ends?"

"We?" he asked, arching an eyebrow at me.

I swallowed. "Yeah, Kent." My voice was so low I didn't even know if he'd be able to hear the words. Or I was just high. Honestly, it could have been either. "We." A smile quirked in the corner of his mouth. Did he really think I'd just leave him behind?

"You'll sing," he said, like he already knew the trajectory of our life. "I'll probably get a job in an office or something."

I took his hand and gave it a squeeze. "Your hands are too precious to get dirty with manual labor."

"You think so?"

"Know so," I said. Below us, Kent's dog, Abe, was barking up a storm, and Kent and I peered over the edge at him. "Just me, you, and our little guy." I wanted to say more. To say he could be like our little baby. The dog I forced Momma to get him because I knew he was sad. I'd never been much of a dog person, but Abe was a sweet little soul. Gentle for gentleness's sake; just like

Kent. When Kent's grandma died the summer before, he'd been inconsolable. Sister Fox had to call Momma and ask her to bring me over to talk to him. I ended up staying the night, cuddling up with him so he knew he was safe. So he knew that he was loved. We might not have said the words, but we didn't ever need to. We both knew. All the way down to our bones, that's how deep it flowed. The next day, I begged Momma to take me to find him a dog. Something he could hold on to when I was at home and he couldn't hold on to me. The day we brought him over, when little Abe peeked his head up over the back window, Kent cried. Sister Fox demanded we take a picture, and Momma forced her way into the shot, even though I wanted it to be just us. Our own little family. One that would get us through the eventual hump of losing our own families when we came out.

"I'd like that," Kent said.

"Then I can sing to you. I will, Kent. I know you like it when I do. Every night, I'll sing your song just so you know you're not alone." I grabbed his hand and squeezed it without holding anything back. "You're never alone. Not when you've got me."

Kent sniffled, and the sound just about broke my heart. I turned and smiled at him, then I wrapped my arm around his back and pulled him in for a hug.

I kissed his shoulder. "We're gonna spend our whole life together, you know?"

"We are?" His voice cracked as he said the words.

"Forever. And then even longer," I said, pointing up at the starry sky. In the distance, they flickered and glittered across the endless blanket of blacks and dark blues. A peppering of whites and golds and even a few pinks twinkling above us. I didn't know what my vision of Heaven was, but I knew Kent would be right there beside me. Even if we just ended up as stardust, shimmers of gas fluttering in the sky, I'd gladly sparkle at his side.

Chapter Five

February 2003

Two months before Kent's eighteenth birthday, we spent the day at our lake. It was too cold for us to swim, but that didn't stop us from building ourselves a campfire and cuddling up close to each other. We laid out a blanket for us to sit on, and another to wrap around us. Kent was leaning against the tree reading a book, and I had my head in his lap, fading in and out of sleep. His fingers were in my hair, and he'd occasionally scratch the back of my scalp. I loved the way his fingers felt there, like it was where they belonged.

At one point, I opened my eyes and realized the sun was setting over the trees. If it was close to dusk, which meant we'd been out there for at least five hours. I remembered we hadn't settled on what movie he was going to sneak us into that weekend. After the debacle with *Scream 2* when I practically crawled into his lap to hide my face, slasher flicks were off the table, but there was one I'd heard about from some of the kids at school.

I rolled onto my back and smiled up at him. "Hey, Half-pint."

He chuckled, his fingers still combing through my hair. "Hey, Gray. You nodded off."

I shook my head. "I was just thinking. On Saturday, I think we should go see that *Walk to Remember* movie."

He groaned. "Mandy Moore is trash."

"You're trash," I teased. "Seriously. It'll be fun. Just think, a Christian. On the big screen, Half-paint. Ain't that something?"

He darted his eyes at me, cocking a brow. "Christians have dominated mainstream media for decades, Grayson."

I rolled my eyes. "I can come pick you up in my truck, and we can go watch it together. Maybe we could get a burger together after, or something." I'd been building myself up to finally have *the talk* with him. The one where we finally admit our feelings out loud. Kent had always been mine, and I had always been his, but I needed to say it out loud because we would never get anywhere if neither of us acknowledged the big gay elephant in the room.

Kent folded the corner of the page he was reading and closed his book. He set it to the side and stared down at me, still playing with my hair. His fingers were tugging harder than they had been, not painfully, but it wasn't necessarily comfortable. A question formed on his lips, but no words came out. He just sat there staring down at me with his mouth hanging open. I reached up, touching his chin with my finger and pushing it closed.

"You'll catch flies that way."

He forced another smile, but I could tell there was something brewing inside of him. Wanting to get the words out, but too scared to actually say them.

"What's wrong?"

He shook his head. "Nothing's wrong. I just ... Kate asked me to go see a movie this weekend."

While I didn't like the way she'd inserted herself into our plans for Saturday, I knew Kent well enough to know if it came to it, he'd tell her no if I asked him to.

"But it's Saturday. Saturday is our day."

"I know, I just ..." He averted his gaze, looking out across the water, now reflecting pinks and oranges like a portrait of Texas at dusk. "I like her." His eyes darted down at me quickly before turning back toward the water.

"I'm not sure what the issue is. We like Kate, don't we? Did that change and I just didn't get the memo?"

Kent sighed, and then he pulled his hand away from my head and twitched his leg, motioning for me to move. I sat up and spun around on my butt, crossing my legs and tucking them together at the ankles. Kent's eyes were still focusing on the water, and I followed his line of sight.

When I looked out at those sparkling swirls of pinks and blues and all that orange, Kent Fox at my side—right where he was meant to be—I felt *Him* there with us. Like our feelings for each other were so big and beautiful that God couldn't tear himself away from the show.

Kent was shaking. His hands. His legs. Tiny tremors that might have gone unnoticed by the untrained eye, but I'd been familiarizing myself with his body since the day we met. I knew his body better than I knew my own. How it reacted to stress. The way it responded to pleasure. His big, brown, puppy-dog eyes and the way they seemed to almost double in size every time we touched.

I couldn't hold them back any longer. The words were rising inside me, demanding release. I'd spent years holding them in, and for what? Kent loved me. He might not have ever said it, but I saw it. I saw him. I *always* saw him.

"Kent, I—"

Our voices crashed into each other, both of us stuttering and sputtering to get our points across, the same way my truck did when it idled in winter.

"I'm taking Kate on a date Saturday."

I laughed. I hadn't meant to, but his words sounded so ridiculous, I couldn't help it. As if Kent would ever go on a date with a girl. And Kate, of all people? I knew he had to be pulling my leg. It had to be some corny joke that was missing its punchline.

"Good one," I said, rolling my eyes. "Seriously, though. Tell Kate she can hang out with us next weekend. It's almost your birthday and we haven't even started planning the party. I was thinking, after the movie, we could—"

"Grayson," he said, his voice sounding distant. Detached. It was like I was talking to a stranger.

The look on his face spoke volumes, and before he had a chance to voice those words out loud, before he could break me in front of him, I shook my head. "You can't be serious. Saturday is our day. You can't—you're not ..." My mouth was hanging open, and every word that left me was jittery and jagged. "It's our day, Kent." He sighed, reaching out to take my hand, but I pulled away from him and jolted to my feet, backstepping away from him.

"It's not a big deal. We can just go—"

"No, we can't," I interrupted, walking a few more steps away. "Because every day it's school and church, school and church, school and freaking church. Monday, church. Tuesday, bible study. Wednesday, prayer meeting. Friday, worship. Sunday, church. Our whole life is the freaking church, Half-pint, and now you're giving her what little time we get to share."

"I don't know what the hell your problem is right now, but you don't have to yell at me. It's just a fucking date, dude."

Whirling around on my heels, I marched toward him. My face must have been a terrifying sight, because he winced as I approached. He stood up and took a step back, bumping into the old oak tree behind him. Bending down, I picked up a handful of dirt and threw it in his face.

"What the fuck, Gray?"

"Watch your dang mouth! I don't know how many times I have to tell you. God help me, if you end up in Hell and I'm stuck in Heaven without you, I'll rip those gates wide open, drag you to this lake, and hold your head underwater until the bubbles stop."

He chuckled, but nothing about this was funny. I bent again, meaning to grab another handful of dirt, but he grabbed my wrist and jerked me back up. He took a step forward. I scowled and took a step back, jerking my arm away and shoving my hand into my pocket.

"First of all, if I'm already dead, I don't think I'll be making any bubbles. And second, I'm pretty sure prison-breaking a damned soul from the flames of Hell is a sin." He was smiling. He was basically pre-confessing to cheating on me, and the jerk was smiling at me like I amused him. Like the simple act of breaking my heart was nothing serious.

I threw my hands in the air. "Then we can burn together. Congratulations, you've just damned my eternal soul, on top of breaking—" I bit my tongue. It was the only way to keep the words in.

He raised an eyebrow at me, that stupid, uninvited smile of his unfaltering. He took a step forward and wrapped his arms around me. "We'll burn beautifully."

I scowled at him and shook my head. "On second thought, how about you take Kate with you into those flames. I'm sure you'll both have a fan-freaking-tastic time down there. You can kiss with your tongues and everything."

"What's gotten into you? You're all over the place, Gray."

"And you're a jerk, but it doesn't stop me from wanting to spend Saturday with you. But screw it, Kent. You take Kate, and I'll just sit my ass at home and wait for you to call and fill me in on the gory details. Is that alright with you? Get matching tattoos. Spend weekends touching all over each other like sex-crazed deviants. Take a stupid picture together with Abe and put it on your Christmas card that you won't bother sending to me because you'll be too far up Kate's butt to remember. So, yeah. Go ahead and take her out this weekend, and then why don't you both just go straight to Hell? How's that for your Christmas card?" He took a step toward me, then another. He kept walking until there was only an inch or two separating us. When he started to speak, I knew only destruction rested in that vicious little mouth of his, and I had no desire to be destroyed. I took another step forward and shoved my palms into his chest, sending him toppling to the ground. I'd never seen a look of absolute betrayal until that moment. Not until Kent stared up at me with shock and horror in his eyes.

"You just pushed me." It felt more like a question than a statement. Like he couldn't believe what I'd just done.

"And you're an asshole. Since we're just stating the facts." I reached into my pocket and fished out my keys before hurling them onto the ground beside him. "Drive your damn self home. I can't even look at you right now."

He called out to me as I walked past the tree line, but tears were hot in my eyes and I couldn't let him see me like that.

Kent had a girlfriend. A girl. It felt like I just caught him cheating on me. Like I walked in on her going down on him. My stomach churned, and when I was out of sight, I needed to sit down behind a tree to catch my breath. It didn't make sense. Not a single bit of sense. Kent was mine. He was mine, and I was his, and he was freaking ruining it.

Light pierced through the canopy of limbs and leaves, and a feeling hit me that scared the heck out of me. Rage. Rage toward God for letting this happen. A deep, bitter anger at Kent for thinking any of this was okay. I glared up at the sky, wanting nothing more than to drag God himself down to earth and beat him up. Punch him in the face. Knee him in the nuts or something. He'd given me Kent Fox on a silver platter and then he'd just taken him away.

"Please, fix this. I ain't never had a bad word to say about you. I've been a good person. Why are you taking him away?" I smashed my palms against my cheeks, shoving away the tears staining my face. "Please, don't take him away from me."

***

After reciting my weekly verse to Sister Thorpe, I practically leapt out of my chair, making my way out of the classroom, through the narrow hallway, toward my supposed best friend. By learning my verses, I'd earned myself an extra twenty-minute break, as had Kent.

He was in the school's cafeteria, which was clearly just the home's dining room before Brother Blankenship repurposed it. Like the rest of the school, nothing about the room was inviting. There was an old picnic table sitting near the door leading out back, and a soda machine that hadn't worked the entire time I'd been there. On the wall, there was a framed photograph of Brother Blankenship standing next to a cardboard cutout of George W. Bush, but aside from that, it was empty.

Kent was alone at the picnic table when I approached. He had a book in his hand, and he was munching on a bag of Cool Ranch Doritos. I paused in the doorway, second-guessing my plan. I was about to break his heart. His big, beautiful heart that was supposed to be beating for me. I shouldn't have taken joy in the fact I was about to ruin a relationship he'd been so happy to start, but I couldn't help it. A smile crept up in the corners of my mouth.

Mid-morning sunlight filtered through the French doors, pouring around him from behind. It almost looked like he was glowing. Like he was an angel sent down to make this world a better, brighter place. Because that's what Kent did. He made everything better. Before I met him, I'd been sad and lonely all the time. He came into my life like a tornado, ripping and ravaging what I knew as fact and replacing it with undeniable proof. There was no shame in how I felt for him. It wasn't wrong—it wasn't a sin—it was just the truth.

I didn't know if he caught sight of me in his peripheral vision, or if he simply felt my gaze tearing through him, but Kent lifted his eyes and found me leaning against the doorframe; arms crossed, barely breathing. He took a gulp of air, and a rush of color flooded his cheeks.

"Hey, Two-liter," he said. His voice was shaky, still startled by my unannounced presence.

I smiled and gave him a quick nod. "Hey, Half-pint."

Without invitation, I moved toward him, stalking my way across the small room and taking the seat right next to him. I knew we were safe for a while. The only other person who'd been attempting to memorize their verses was Kyle, and the kid had the brainpower of a dang five-year-old. I scooted my chair right beside him and leaned against him, resting my head on his shoulder.

"You okay?" he asked.

I peered up expecting to see a smile, but Kent had a sullen look on his face that I couldn't quite read. I could have spent hours trying to rationalize that look away in my mind. Days could be dedicated to understanding its meaning. Unfortunately, I didn't have days to do so, just twenty minutes before our extra break was over and then we'd be back in that classroom, surrounded by unfriendly faces and a girl I hated with every fiber of my being. She was trying to take what was mine. That wasn't going to happen.

I realized he was still staring at me, questions coursing through his eyes, and it dawned on me that he was still waiting for an answer.

I shook my head.

"What's wrong?" he squeezed my hand, the way he used to before she came into the picture.

"Just missing you, I guess."

He smiled, but I couldn't tell if it was genuine. He'd been so distant lately. It was almost like he didn't understand why I might be sad after he took our time together and made it theirs. Why going from having him at my side every day—eclipsing everything and everyone—to spending scarce moments together in empty church hallways, might have broken my heart.

"Can I ask you a question?" I said.

"You can ask me anything. You know that."

I didn't, actually. I didn't know that at all. Two months before, I thought I did, but things had changed. Our bond shifted. He was hers now, and I had to watch it all unfold in our tiny classroom. He held her hand in front of me like I was nothing to him. Like I'd been nothing to him all along.

"If you knew someone was trying to hurt me, you'd want to protect me, wouldn't you?"

His eyes narrowed into small slits and he clenched his fist. "Is someone picking on you? Who is it? Tommy?"

"It's just a hypothetical question. No one's trying to hurt me. But if they were, you'd try to help, right?"

"Of course, I would."

"What if it was somebody I was close to. Someone I was supposed to trust."

"Just spit it out Two-liter. Who's trying to hurt you?"

I took a deep breath to steady myself. I knew this could go one of two ways. This was Kate. His girlfriend. As much as the title pained me to say, it was true.

"I think Kate's cheating on you."

He stared at me. Every nerve in my body was shouting out warning signals of *don't-don't-don't,* but I couldn't listen to them. Not at that moment. Not with this silver bullet locked and loaded, trained on a wolf with terrific taste in men and treachery in her heart.

"Why do you think she's cheating on me?" His face was steady, not a single bit of emotion on it. I couldn't read him like I used to, and that scared the heck out of me. Still, I knew I had to do this. If I wanted Kate out of the picture, this was my only chance.

"I heard her talking to someone in the bathroom earlier. She was telling him she wanted to take him somewhere ..." I swallowed down the anger rising up in me like bile. "Somewhere private to do stuff with him." I winced as the words left me, and I couldn't stand to see Kent's face anymore, so I stared down at my hands. "Sex stuff, Kent."

"Sex stuff?"

I nodded. "Said she wanted to ride him like a bucking bronco, whatever the heck that means."

"Did she now?" Kent gripped the arms of his chair, tapping his fingers against the metal. "And who is this mystery man?"

I shrugged. "Don't know. Didn't stay long enough to find out."

"So, you were in the bathroom when she said this?"

"Yeah."

"The single bathroom; one toilet, a shower, and a sink. That's the bathroom you heard her say it in?"

Dang. Dang, dang, dang. Gosh, this was a terrible idea. In my fit of madness, I'd forgotten that our school was still just a converted three-bedroom house. There wasn't a single school-like thing about it. Not the bedrooms-turned-classrooms. Not the kitchen-slash-dining-room-turned-break-room. Definitely not the small bathroom. None of it.

"I was hiding in the shower," I attempted, reaching into his bag of chips and stealing a Dorito. "You know I've been worried about the math test at the end of my workbook. I just wanted some time to hype myself up for it before Sister Thorpe—"

"And you hid in the shower?" he interrupted. "Then Kate came in with a mystery man and started detailing the dirty stuff she wanted to do to him?"

"Pretty much."

"In the shower without a shower curtain. That's where you were hiding? Were you just lying down real low or were you wearing your cloak of invisibility?"

"Please don't mention Harry Potter. You know witchcraft makes me nervous. And there's something about J.K. Rowling that doesn't sit right, either. She's an odd duck."

"Dammit, Grayson. Stop." He jerked his shoulder away, breaking the connection the side of my face had with him. "What the hell is your problem? You're acting like she's abusive toward me or something. All this extra stuff you're doing, it's creepy."

It felt like he'd slapped me in the face. "You think I'm creepy?"

He sighed, reaching over and squeezing my knee. "I'm sorry. I didn't mean that. It's just a lot. Between trying to find time to split between you and Kate, and all the hours we spend at church, it's like I'm burning the candle at both ends. I'm exhausted, and now you're making up some story because you're jealous that I have someone that's not you to talk to. But I can't keep doing it, Gray. I'm tired." He pinched the bridge of his nose and sighed. "I'm so fucking tired of feeling tired. And I'm trying to fix it, but you're just ..." He shook his head, stopping himself before he said something he couldn't take back.

"Fix what?" I asked, taking a step forward. "What are you trying to fix? What the heck does that even mean? We ain't broken, Half-pint."

He looked over his shoulder, and for the first time in a long time, I saw the boy I knew. The boy I loved. "I wish that was true. You don't know how much I wish that was true." He grabbed his empty bag of chips and shuffled slowly toward the trash can, shoving the wrapper inside. With his back to me, I was able to breathe again. So long as I couldn't see the resentment storming in his eyes or hear the hurt in his voice, I could pretend like nothing had changed. That he hadn't taken back what he'd given me willingly. That he didn't even seem to care it was killing me.

It felt like he was slipping away. I could feel our tether stretching to its limit, and I panicked, blurting, "She only wants you because your daddy's the pastor. She don't care about you, Kent. She doesn't love you." Not like me. She could never love him like me.

"This isn't fair, Two-liter. You're my best friend. You're supposed to have my back, but you're just making everything worse."

I had to swallow the sob that was creeping up my throat. Those words; those nasty, hurtful words of his slashed at me, cutting me until I was little more than ribbons of eviscerated skin.

"I'm trying to look out for you," I said, trying to harden my voice. The last thing I needed was to crack in front of him. I wouldn't be able to explain away the tears. Not with him. He'd know. He'd take one look at my heartbroken face, and he would know how I felt. The big secret. The one that had been threatening to steal him away since those feelings settled into my soul.

"If you want to help me, you'll stop this. Grayson, I can't lose ..." his voice trailed off into the most pained sigh I'd ever heard. Without so much as a second glance, he walked past the trash can, through the hallway, and back into the classroom, leaving me all alone. Again.

***

A week passed since I blew up on Kent in the lonely lunchroom. Since then, I did my best to ignore him, hoping it would make him see sense. That he'd realize what he was missing when I wasn't there to smile at him or sing his special song.

It wasn't working.

Kent Fox had a habit, and it was one I loved. When he finished his workbook, he'd swivel his chair to the right, give me that big goofy grin of his, and call out "I win!" despite neither of us being in competition with each other.

He hadn't done it all week.

I mean, he had, but instead of swiveling to the right, he now turned to the left. Toward *her*.

He had to know what he was doing to me. What he was putting me through. I didn't know if he was doing it on purpose, but every time, it felt like a betrayal.

He also had a habit of whispering things to her. Probably saying something super charming. Then they'd grin, and both burst into laughter. Or she'd just give him those stupid flirty eyes of hers that made me want to puke.

Friday afternoon, about an hour before school let out for the weekend, I overheard them making plans. He said he was going to take her out somewhere special. That he had something he needed to tell her.

My chest ached.

She smiled, beaming at him like he'd hung the dang moon, and she told him he could take her anywhere.

He could take her straight to Hell for all I cared.

Kent didn't even tell me goodbye before he left. He just gave me a clipped nod, like I was a stranger on the street.

I walked into the woods Friday night, feeling lower than I ever had. I made my way toward the lake. It had been weeks since we spent an evening together, and I knew the time was coming. The day I'd finally have to let him go, just like he'd done with me.

I sat in front of an old pine tree and pulled my legs to my chest. I wanted to go out to the lake—to our spot—but that felt impossible. It was ours, mine and his, back when we were still an *us*. Not officially or anything, but Kent and I didn't need officiality. What we shared was true. Truer than anything. Maybe even truer than God. It didn't feel right to go to the lake alone. To radiate in the moon's light reflecting back at me from the water. Water I'd spent the last four years wading with Kent.

"I need you," I whispered, unsure if I was talking to God or the memory of Kent. The boy with tangled hair who taught me to dance. The person he was before giving Kate the one thing that was meant for me. "I need you so much it hurts."

There was laughter in the distance. Far-away voices that traveled toward me on the wind. I followed them, figuring it might be Trevor and his buddies. Trevor didn't like when I tagged along with him and his friends, but I was too close to breaking to worry about making him mad. I needed something.

Someone.

Anyone.

The voices grew louder as I approached the clearing. There was a muffled man's voice, but there was a distinct sound of moaning coming from the other side of those trees. The voice was light, almost airy, so I knew it wasn't Trevor. His voice carried enough bass in it that it could double as an instrument during Sunday service. I tried to rack my brain and think of who the heck even knew about the spot—*our spot*—but I kept coming up empty. It wasn't until I stood behind the pine tree closest to the lake that they came into view.

My stomach dropped.

No.

Kent.

My Kent.

He was lying on his back, hands stiff at his sides, as Kate knelt beside him, her fingers touching a place she had no gosh-dang right touching. The full moon hanging overhead lit them up like a spotlight, making every touch—every single stroke—visible to me. It played out like a movie. The worst movie.

Kent's mouth was hanging open like he was trying to speak, but nothing came out. He was a silent symphony, his quiet song of pleasure—a song he was meant to sing for me—ripping my heart in half as it echoed across the still water.

He was enjoying it. Kent was enjoying her.

I had to turn around. They were at *our* spot. The one I found for him. For us. It had been our refuge from the prying eyes of West Clark and all her hateful citizens. The place where we could just exist. Not as Christians. Not as the pastor's son and his clingy best friend. It was the place where I was his and he was mine. Of all the places he could have brought her, why did he have to bring her there?

I turned around, because this wasn't a party I'd been invited to. Behind me, Kent Fox was naked from the waist down. Any other time, I might have kept watching, just to admire his beauty from afar. We were on my father's land, but my heart held no jurisdiction. He moaned, and I bit my own tongue to stifle the sob rising up in my throat. Eventually, curiosity got the better of me.

She pumped him, her hand gliding up and down with no real precision at all. She was sloppy, and I couldn't understand why he was allowing it to happen. I didn't know why he was bucking his hips into the air to meet her touch. He was mine. He was mine, and he was ruining everything.

He called out her name when his release finally found him. It hurt more than everything else combined.

I stayed until they left, my back turned, hands over my ears to drown them out, unsuccessfully blinking back tears. When they drove away in her car, I walked to our spot—the one I'd found just for him—and I knelt in the place where Kent found his pleasure just a few moments ago. The dirt was still warm. From him. Because of him.

"God, please. I don't ask you for much, but I'm asking you for this," I whispered. There were no tingles. No chills running up or down my spine. "I know Kent's daddy says people like us are wrong. That we're an offense to you." I stared up at the sky, searching for God. "But I don't offend you, do I? I'm good enough, ain't I? Am I still worthy to walk in your light?"

God said nothing, the same way Momma didn't say much when I'd tell her about things going on in my life. God was there—I knew he was—but he was ignoring me.

"It's not fair. I do everything you ask, but you're taking the only person who matters to me. What did I ever do that was so bad you thought I deserved this?" I flung my arm to the spot where Kate ravaged him moments earlier. "We were everything. *He* was everything, and now you're taking him away."

It started slowly. Like a soft buzz in the tips of my fingers before it spread through my hands. I raked my finger through the dirt beneath me, my fingers sliding through something sticky and cold.

I cried. Probably harder than I ever had before.

Still, my fingers moved, dancing through dirt like a debutant at the cotillion. My fingertips tapped and tugged through sand mixed with Half-pint's semen, and a soft flame sparked inside of me. It was warmth. A cozy comfort that pressed past my palms, up my arms, and across my chest.

Verses crept through my mind.

My hands twirled through the sludge I created, writing without reason. Looking down, it said, Luke 11:9.

We'd just learned it the week before. Maybe it was still fresh in my mind from Pastor Fox's sermon, or maybe it was God working through me. I didn't know. Didn't really care one way or the other.

And I say unto you, ask, and it shall be given you; seek and ye shall find; knock, and it shall be opened unto you.

I stared at the sky, tears trickling down my cheeks. "Please," I pleaded, my voice hoarse from crying. "Please?"

Chapter Six

April 2003

I don't know if I'd ever been more nervous than I was when we got to the lake that night. Kent sang along with Spice Girls on my truck's stereo the entire ride. He couldn't hold a note to save his life, but his voice was still the most beautiful thing I'd ever heard.

My stomach was spinning when we pulled up. I knew what I had to do—the words I needed him to hear—but the thought of saying them out loud overwhelmed me. Earlier, Trevor asked me if I wanted to go to his buddy Tommy's house to watch some scary movie Momma wouldn't let us watch at home, but Tommy had always been a jerk to me at school—always giving me dirty looks when he caught me staring at Kent, and he was silently judging me for it—so he was the last person I wanted to hang out with.

I don't even know if my truck had come to a complete stop before I jumped out the door and ran toward our spot. I didn't wait for Kent because I knew one look into his big brown eyes would put a proverbial pin in what I was planning on admitting. As scared as I was of his reaction, the fear of letting him go without him knowing what he meant to me was overwhelming. I'd spent the last two months breaking in front of him. I needed him to either put me back together or let me shatter completely.

My shirt and jeans came off first, then my socks. I sprinted into the water, with Kent trailing slowly behind me. Once I was waist-deep, I turned around and held my arm out for him.

"Kent," I said, my eyes tearing into him like a Christmas present. He jogged toward me, pulling his shirt over his head and throwing it behind himself. He watched me watching him, and I made no attempt to hide what I was doing.

This was it. All or nothing. I wouldn't look away from him. If he hated me after the words were out, then so be it. I wasn't leaving the lake without telling Kent I loved him.

Once his pants were off, Kent walked into the water and swam toward me wearing only his boxer-briefs. I couldn't handle the sight of him approaching; It was just too much. Too many nerves, not enough courage. I just needed a moment. Diving under the water, I circled him, swimming around aimlessly. I swam lower to the bottom, reaching over to tickle his feet.

"No, Gray, don't. I hate when you do—argh, fuck!" His voice was muffled through the water, but I heard every word. I swam circles around him, my fingers exploring him freely. Tickling every exposed patch of skin I could find.

When I opened my eyes, I was behind him. His butt was right there. Just within reach. If this was it—if this was my last chance, I was going to take it. I reached for him, sliding my hand against his cheek. It was perfect. Just like I knew it would be. Soft and jiggly. Gosh, I wanted to feel his skin. Touch the light dusting of hair I knew grew under the fabric.

I took in a mouthful of lake water and swam around until I was in front of him. I popped out of the water like a lake-living Jack-in-the-box. Pursing my lips, I spat the water directly into his face.

This was it. I'd caught him off guard.

All or nothing. For Kent. For us.

"I hate you. God, I hate—"

I reached for him. He needed to know I could love him better than Kate. That I could give him what she couldn't. I was his Two-liter, and I loved him with everything I had in me. He had to know. The second my hand came into contact with his bulge, he stopped talking. His eyes doubled in size, and …

I knew it! I freaking knew it!

He was smiling. Gosh, he was smiling so big.

More than that, he was getting hard, the way I got when I thought about him at night in bed. I touched him the way I liked to touch myself, tracing his length with my finger. Up and down, pausing at the curve where his shaft shifted into the head. I flicked my finger against that bump over and over until his whole body was shaking.

Our eyes met, and I smiled at him. "Hey," I whispered.

"Hey," Kent said, paddling even closer. "Hey, Gray."

He wanted this. I knew he did. I'd always known. And finally, I was making him feel good, but he needed more. He needed to know what I was willing to give him, and just how gone on him I already was. My fingertips teetered on the edge of the elastic waistband separating him from me. I wanted to rip them off and take him in my hand completely, but I needed his permission first. I tapped his hip like I was knocking on a door.

Kent's arms looped around me, pulling me closer, then he nodded. Reaching inside, I wrapped my hand around it and stroked.

This was it. The moment of truth.

"I want you to break up with Kate," I said, trying to keep my voice steady.

"You do?"

"I do, and I've got a list of seventeen reasons why you should."

His head tilted back, and he let out a moan. Louder than the one he'd given Kate a few nights back. With his eyes closed, he said, "That's—Jesus, Gray—that's nice."

I arched an eyebrow at him. "Is it?"

"So ... so nice." He bucked his hips forward, grinding himself into my palm. "Tell me. Tell me why. Your list ... tell me about your list." I wanted to lean forward and take him by the tongue. Invade every inch of his mouth and claim it for myself. I resisted that urge, because I needed an answer.

"All seventeen?" I asked.

"All of them. All of it. Let me have all of it. Just the ... just, yeah. God, Gray. Just like that." As I stroked him with one hand, I snaked the other around his back, grabbing his butt. He twitched against my thigh, rocking his hips forward, seeking even more contact.

"Well, first of all, I hate her."

He chuckled. "That's definitely a reason."

I tried to hide the sound of my sniffle. He was too wrapped up in his erection to notice, thankfully. "Second, I miss you."

His eyes sprung open like I'd just sent a stream of static directly into his heart. "You do?"

"Of course, I do. This is the first time I've seen you in a week. You promised me you would still make time for me. When you two started seeing each other, you swore it. You can't just forget about me. You promised." I was getting angry. Even though he was humping my hand, and even though I knew he wanted this just as much as I did, it hurt to think about the way he'd discarded me. How easy it had been for him to let me go. When I stopped stroking him, he thrust forward, seeking friction. "You hurt me, Half-pint. You've been hurting me this whole time."

"Sorry," he said between his panting. "So sorry. Didn't mean ... I didn't ..."

I shook my head, tightening the grip I had on his erection. "Third, I don't know what you two do when I'm not around, and I don't like it."

"What do you mean?" His voice was shaky. Like we were walking on quaking ground that was crumbling around us, threatening to swallow us whole.

I squeezed it even harder. "You know what I mean."

His eyes widened. "I wouldn't. We haven't—"

"Don't lie to me." I let go of him. Pulling my hands out of his underwear, I did a couple of backstrokes to put some distance between us. As much as I wanted it—wanted him—I wouldn't sit there and let him lie to my face. "We don't lie to each other."

"I'm not."

I stared out at the water, watching the stars' reflections glittering against the rippling waves. "I love this place, you know. Our place. It's still ours, isn't it?"

"It always has been." Kent paddled forward to get to me, but I held my hand up and shook my head. I needed him to be honest with me, the way I planned on being with him.

"Have you slept with her?"

His eyes bulged, and he shook his head frantically, like it might make it all better somehow. "No. I wouldn't. I promise."

"Why?"

"Why what?"

"She's your girlfriend, Kent. Why wouldn't you have sex with her?"

"Why are you bringing this up right now? Just come back here." He tried flagging me forward, motioning for me to come back to him, but I couldn't. I needed to hear it first. "Please, come back."

As the image of him bucking up into her hand filled my mind, anger bubbled up inside of me like boiling water on the stove. The longer he floated in front of me, doubling down on his lie, the closer that anger bubbled toward the surface, ready to spill over. "Why wouldn't you let her rub her hands all up and down on you? She's your girlfriend. Why wouldn't you bring her here?" I jerked my head back in his direction, staring him dead in the eyes. "To our spot, the one I found just for *us*, and lay down under that tree right there, and let her do ..." I slammed my hand back into his underwear and stroked him once, root to tip. "This."

"Were you following us?" Kent's entire body went rigid. "So, you ... what? Followed us out here and just watched us from the shadows? What the hell?"

"Don't try to turn this around on me. I'm not the one who was—"

"Why do you care? Huh? Why does it matter what I did with her?"

"You know why!" I let go of him and floated back, trying to put space between us. He didn't seem to care that I didn't want him near me, because he met every one of my backstrokes with a lunge forward. "Break up with her. Do it tonight."

"Tell me why. If you want me to leave her, I want to know why."

"I just ... I miss you."

He came even closer, not stopping until he was right in front of me. The anger in his face had faded, melting and morphing into a look that took my breath away. He was desperate. Grasping at every possible straw to get me back to him. To make it right. "Please? Please, just tell me why. I promise, it's okay."

I stared down at my reflection in the water, not recognizing the man looking back. I remembered our life together. Quiet lunches at school, sharing Pringles and cookies from Bronson's Bakery. Kent teaching me dance moves in his bedroom. The stolen glances. Our lingering touches. The way his lips felt when he poured smoke into my lungs. His hands. Gosh, his hands exploring me freely, his touch hot and full of raw, undeniable love.

"Do you love me, Kent?" My voice cracked, and I knew if he said no, it would end me. I'd sink down in that lake and make no effort to pull myself back up. Because a life without Kent Fox? Not interested. Not in the slightest.

"You're my best friend," he answered, stroking my cheek. "Of course, I love you."

I sighed, wiping away a falling tear. "Not like that. Not just ... not just like a friend, Half-pint." I'd said it. The words I planned on saying. The admission I would never be able to take back. I loved him, and now he knew it. Kent struggled to breathe, each exhale accompanied with a cracked wheeze. I looked up at him, staring him right in the eyes, and mouthed, *"Please?"*

Whatever he was struggling with, whichever battles he was waging in that beautiful head of his, they faded. Erased from existence with a long, beautiful exhale.

"Is it okay if I do?"

I nodded, hoping he'd say it so I didn't have to. The longer we sat there, the more nervous I became. I tried to speak the words softly, but they came out in a frenzy; panic and passion and pure terror mixed together. A cake baked with confusion; my love sprinkled on top to make it pretty. "What do you think this is? Everything I've been saying, all of this, it's because of you. Because of how I feel about you." He opened his mouth to speak, but I covered it with my hand. I was there. Right where he needed me. He was scared, and I could take that fear away from him. All it would take were three words I'd whispered in my head more times than I could count.

He kissed my palm.

"It's because I love you," I admitted. "Is it okay?" I scoffed at him, letting him see just how silly that question had been. "I guess it doesn't have to be okay. It just has to be true. It's true for me. Truer than anything. Truer than Texas. Truer than God, even." I took a deep breath. If this was it—our beginning—I needed him to know what he'd put me through. Just how lost I'd felt without him. "I love you, Half-pint. Deep down in my soul, I love you. I thought you loved me back. Up until two months ago, I thought that we were ..."

"Thought we were what?"

"I thought it was going to be you and me." I shoved my hand forward, shoving him right in the heart, the same way he'd been pushing mine around the whole time. "It's supposed to be you and me, but you're ruining it. I thought you loved me back. This is killing me. You hold her hand in front of me. Do you know what that does to me? I want ... I want it to be my hand. I want it to be my hand you're holding so bad. Seeing you with her here, in our place, watching her slide her hand all over you—" I slammed my hand against my mouth. Damn. Damn, damn, damn. He'd already accused me of stalking him, and there I was, admitting it. "I wasn't following you. I've been coming out here every night because I miss you so dang much." Tears were falling down my cheeks and I reached up to wipe them away. He watched my every move. Every teardrop being shoved out of existence. "Why did you have to let her touch you?"

"I was scared you didn't feel that way about me. That you were catching on. I just didn't want to lose you. Even if this was all we could have, just our friendship, it was enough for me. It was more than enough."

"It isn't enough for me. It's never been. And now she's ... I wanted to be your first. To be your only, 'cause you were gonna be mine."

"I was?" He sounded like he was about to cry. But that wasn't what I wanted. I didn't want him to feel as sad and lonely as I had been. "I want to be, I swear. What you just did to me, how you just made me feel, I've been waiting for that, Gray. I've been praying for that. For you. I don't like girls, not any of them."

"You don't?"

"I've been hoping for you for so long," he said, tugging my chin so I was looking at him again. He cupped my face with his hand and smiled so big, I thought it might just be the death of me. "I love you. Would it be alright—I mean, would you mind if I ..." He closed his eyes, touching his forehead to mine. "Kiss me?"

Our mouths opened, and he sucked in my bottom lip, kissing me gently. His fingers combed through my wet hair, tapping the crown of my head twice before dragging them gently down until his hand was wrapped around the nape of my neck.

"Say it again," Kent whispered. "Please, Gray?"

"I love you." Our lips touched, then parted. Kent opened, as if he was splitting himself wide-open, just for me. It was like all of our lives we'd been working toward this moment, and with something as simple as allowing me entry, he was walking us into our future. It was everything I thought it would be. More. It was so much more than I'd hoped for. More than I could have even dreamed. "I love you," I whispered. "I love you, I love you, I love you, Kent Fox."

***

The darkened light in Momma's window told me she was sleeping by the time we got back to the house. Good. What we planned to do—the things I planned to do to him—I didn't need her knocking on the door in the middle of what was about to happen.

I led Kent upstairs, his hands exploring my exposed skin every step of the way. God. This was really happening. Kent was mine. He was finally mine, and now he knew I'd always been his. I felt dizzied by the revelation. Once we were in my room, he closed my door behind us. I made my way to the bed, pulling my shirt over my head and kicking off my pants. Standing in just my boxer-briefs, I faced him, standing on the other side of the bed. His back was against the door, leaning against it and eying me up and down like he was drinking in the sight of me. I blushed, because I'd never had anyone look at me the way he was. Like I wasn't just a lanky little kid who still got pimples at the slightest sign of sweat.

"Hey," I whispered.

"Grayson," he said. "You're sure? About this. Us?" He winced. "About me?"

Did he still not believe me? Because I was just as deep in this as he was. I'd always been. So I hooked my thumbs in the elastic band of my underwear, hands shaking so hard I didn't know if I'd be able to actually push them down. I waited for his approval—for permission—to introduce myself to him in that way. The way I'd thought about it, every night, in the bed I was standing in front of. Ever since I learned what happened when I twisted and tugged at it.

Kent licked his lips and reached for the bottom of his shirt, pulling it over his head.

I'd seen him shirtless more times than I could count, but something about that moment, seeing him stripping himself down, readying himself for me, it was like an explosion. Thousands of bottle rockets shooting fireworks up into the Texas sky. His pants came off next, and there he was. Standing on the other side of the bed, damp white boxer-briefs that showed every curve and every crook. My eyes lingered on his bulge, wanting to see my Half-pint bare. I'd only ever seen it once, all those years ago in his bedroom after we danced our hearts out to the Spice Girls. When I goaded him about his size to hide the fact that he just turned my entire world upside down.

At the lake, when I had my hand around it, it pulsed and twitched at my touch. I did that to him. He'd practically spilled over right there in the lake.

I climbed onto my bed, hobbling forward on my knees and holding my arms out toward him. "Half-pint." The words couldn't have been louder than a whisper, but he mustn't have needed much more than that. He climbed onto the bed and crawled toward me, stopping when we were chest to chest. His thumb brushed against my cheek, and I knew that if this was the end—even if this were my last night on this earth—this thing we were sharing would be the defining moment of my life.

His lips ghosted mine, landing firmly on my jaw and leaving a trail of kisses up the side of my face. "Gray," he moaned, light and low. "I've wanted this for so long." He pressed his lips against my neck, his hand brushing through my hair. "This is real? You're not just—"

"I love you!" I blurted. "You don't even know, Kent. You don't even know." My hands were ... Gosh, they were everywhere. Touching his shoulders. His back. His butt. I squeezed his cheeks in my hand, just needing to feel them. The warmth of his skin. The light dusting of hair that grew on his beautiful backside.

"I'm in this. Me and you, Kent. I ain't ever wanted anyone or anything more than I want you."

He wrapped his arms around my back and pulled me close to him. "How long have you known?" Another kiss against my shoulder was all I needed to guide me through it.

"You taught me to dance. Kent, I didn't know. Not what it meant, at least, but I knew you meant something to me. That you were special."

He pulled away, tears fresh in his eyes. I reached up and brushed them away, kissing the damp splotches of skin as if I could magically kiss away his upset. "Jesus, Two-liter. We were thirteen. You loved me all that time?"

I nodded. "You remember when you asked me which Spice Girl was my favorite?"

"Yeah. Emma, wasn't it?"

"Baby," I corrected. "The way you said it, I thought you were saying it to me. I thought that's what you were calling me."

Kent laughed, which just made me feel embarrassed. Like I'd just made some big dating blunder in front of him. I looked down, but his hand just found my chin and lifted it right back up.

"You are. You always have been," he whispered.

We slid our underwear down, and counted out loud, down from three. When I opened my eyes, he was there. Right in front of me, not a strip of fabric to hide behind.

"Oh, my God," I said, because the sight of him, seeing him hard like that, knowing I was the reason, I'd risk a little blasphemy for that. Every inch of him was perfect.

I lay back on the bed, fully exposed. Pulling my legs up to my chest; the same way I'd seen in the magazine I'd swiped from the bookstore the year before, leaving twenty bucks Daddy gave me for helping him on the farm in its place. "Please, Kent?" Pausing to wipe a tear away. "I've wanted this for so long. I've been aching for you, and you can make that ache stop. Please?"

"Grayson, I love you," he whispered, running his fingers up and down my thighs. "I'm sorry I hurt you with Kate." He reached up and brushed a tear away. "I swear to God, if I knew—"

"I know," I said, because I did. Of course, he'd never hurt me. Of course, he wouldn't. I took his hand and guided him to me, wrapping his fist around my shaft. "Make me yours."

"If you don't mind," he said, making his way even closer. "There are a few other things I'd like to do first."

I cocked my head to the side. "Other things?"

He nodded. "Put your legs down and let me show you." Trusting him, I did as he asked, stretching my legs out and keeping them spread wide. He settled between them, eyes locked on the prize. "You don't know how long I've wanted this, Grayson."

"I do, because I wanted it, too."

He moved closer, his hand on my cheek, lips brushing gently with mine. "I love you. I'm gonna love you for the rest of my life, Gray Collins." He ran his fingers through my hair. "Until we're old and gray."

I snorted a laugh. "That's the corniest line I've ever heard."

"Whatever. The point remains—I'm yours. I'm yours for as long as you'll have me."

I pressed our foreheads together. "Forever?"

"That's what you want?"

I nodded. "Yeah. Yeah, Kent. I want forever."

"Deal." He kissed his way down my jaw, not stopping when he reached my neck. His lips twisted and tugged against my skin, suckling like he was trying to draw blood. The whole time he was sucking my neck, his fingers grazed my nipples, making me whimper like a love-starved kitten.

"Hush, baby. You'll wake them up."

"Sorry," I whispered.

He looked up with a goofy grin, and I wanted to tangle my fingers through those adorable curls. God. Why did he have to be so beautiful? Why did it have to feel so right? His lips ventured lower, leaving a trail of slick saliva as he made his way to my nipple. He wrapped his lips around the hardened nub, making me whine in pleasure. He shot me another pleading look, so I bit my bottom lip, just trying to keep myself from making more noise.

"I've been thinking." I raked my fingers through his curls, really feeling them for the first time. They'd always been my favorite thing about Kent, aside from his butt, and having free rein over them without worrying about him figuring out my hidden feelings—it felt like being given the world.

"After school ends, I think we should leave town."

He looked up at me, seeming dazed, his lips wrapped around my nipple. When he pulled away, there was an audible wet pop, and the smacking sound sent a rush of blood surging to my penis, now aching against Kent's side.

"Why?" he asked, blinking slowly.

"They'll never let us be happy, Half-pint. What we are is an affront to everything our families believe. Your momma might be okay with it, but your dad would kill us."

Kent nodded, looking more resigned to his fate than anything. There wasn't any hope on his face, but when I gently tugged his curls, it pulled him back into the moment, and a smile spread across his face.

"It's okay," he finally said. "If I lose them, it's okay, because I'll still have you."

"You'll always have me." Then I placed a finger under his chin and lifted it until our gazes met. "I'm going to take care of you, Half-pint. I'm going to make sure you never have to want for anything again, I promise. You ain't gotta be scared." I leaned down and softly kissed him, our lips working slowly, like we were trying to memorize every inch of each other. "You ain't ever gotta be scared again, Kent."

He nodded, his eyes getting a little mistier. "It's just, I've been so scared of losing you, Grayson. I know I hurt you with Kate, but I only did it because I was trying to keep you in my life. I thought maybe I could fix myself to stop from losing you. You know that, don't you? I—" His voice cracked, and I could tell he was just as close to breaking all over, so I pulled him to me, holding him right against my chest. "I can't lose you, Two-liter. I can't ever lose you."

"You won't. It's me and you now. Forever. Now that I know you want this, too, you're never getting rid of me."

He sniffles, drying his eyes as he looks up at me. "Promise?"

I nodded, meaning it more than I'd ever meant anything. "I swear."

"Good." He swallowed, pulling away and staring down at my penis. "Can I suck you, Gray? Please? I'll be careful with my teeth. I've been practicing."

I arched an eyebrow. "You've been practicing?"

His cheeks turned the shade of a stop sign. "Yeah. With a toy. I bought it and had it sent through the mail from one of those dirty infomercials that play at night."

"A toy? You bought—you mean, like an adult toy?" I asked. A smile quirked in the corners of his mouth and he nodded like he was proud of himself. For buying a dang dildo, no less! Good grief. If his parents found it, they'd kill him.

"It's shaped like a cock." Gosh. The way he said the word made it sound so tawdry. "I like to imagine it's your cock, Grayson." It was my turn to blush, and I must have looked like a scandalized virgin—mainly because that's exactly what I was—because his smirk just grew even wider. "In my head, I've sucked your cock at least a hundred times. I've even imagined you fucking me."

"Good Lord," I whispered, feeling a little breathless. "You shouldn't talk like that." Whatever resistance I may have been holding onto faded the moment he wrapped his hand around my shaft and stroked me slowly.

"Is that what you want, baby? Do you want to fuck me?"

"Jesus," I whimpered. "Yeah. Yeah, Kent. Wanna ... wanna *fuck* you." Just saying the word made me feel like the biggest sinner this side of Dallas, but I pushed past that nervousness, because I was with Kent, and I knew I was always safe with him. "I stare at your butt all the time. Love it. Want to touch it. Squeeze it."

"Would you want to kiss it?"

I looked into his eyes, blinking slowly, confused. "Huh?" He dragged his finger down my lips, pupils blown wide as I opened my mouth, welcoming him in. I shelled my tongue around him, wanting to taste him.

"Would you want to kiss it?" he repeated. "With your tongue, maybe?"

I tried to picture what he was suggesting, but the mental image didn't make sense. Using every ounce of my self-control, I released his finger from my mouth and pulled away.

"You want me to lick your butt?"

"So fucking much," he breathed.

"So, I'd what? ... Just lick your butt cheek?" Okay, well ... I didn't really hate the idea, it just seemed like a strange request.

He shook his head. "Inside the crack. Against my butthole, I guess. I watched one of those nasty movies a few months ago. They were getting ready to do the dirty, and he knelt back there, spread those cheeks, and dove right in." He wasn't blushing or anything, and I had to give him credit for that. My cheeks, on the other hand, were practically scorching. I felt lightheaded at the implication. "It was a man and a woman, so I don't know if it's something two guys would do together, but I wouldn't mind. Would you want to do that?"

"L-lick your b-butthole?" I clarified, stumbling and tumbling over my words.

"Yeah. Or I could lick yours. I just thought it looked hot. You'd look gorgeous bent over in front of me like that."

"Can I try it later? I'm sorry, Half-pint, I'm trying to wrap my head around what we're about to do, adding butts and tongues into the equation sounds a little extreme for our first time."

Tears welled up in his eyes, and I worried I hurt his feelings, so I opened my mouth to apologize, but he cut me off, whispering, "Our first time. We're really doing this, aren't we?"

"We are."

He nodded. "Okay. Yeah, Gray. We've got all the time in the world for the rest." He knelt in front of me, taking me in his hand and slowly stroking. "I'm going to suck you now. Just lie back and relax. Tell me if I'm not doing any good, and I'll try to do better."

I reach down and cup his cheek. "You're going to be great, and even if you aren't, it's okay. Just getting to be this way with you is enough for me."

"Thanks. Okay, here goes nothing." He opened his mouth, and it felt like hours before his lips finally wrapped around the head, making me whimper. Slowly, he descended, his lips like velvet around the shaft. It was like the warmest, wettest hug known to man, and I wanted to feel more of it.

"Kent," I whimpered when he did this neat little trick with his tongue. "More?"

His head bobbed up and down, his cheeks hollowing each time he pulled back. It was like he was sucking the orgasm out of me by force, his fingers gently caressing my balls, one finger venturing further back, playing with the soft, hairless patch of skin between my balls and my crack.

The bed creaked as he maneuvered himself around. I didn't realize what he was doing until we were in a sixty-nine position, and his penis was aimed right at my mouth. I wanted to make him feel good, the same way he'd been doing for me. Leaning closer, I wrapped my lips around him, tasting the salty bead of pre-cum pearled at the tip. The taste was like an explosion of the man I loved. The boy with tangled curls who looked at me like I was the sun and moon and every star in the sky.

I mumbled bastardized variations of "I love you" as I worked him faster, swallowing more and more of my Half-pint. He wasn't terribly large, maybe a little over five inches, but each inch felt like a mile by the time it was hitting the back of my throat. I kept gagging around it, but Kent was a natural. I guessed all that practice with his toy had been helpful. Maybe I could get one for myself, I thought. That way I'd be just as good for him as he was for me.

Kent's warmth left my shaft, making me whine like a needy puppy. Pulling himself out of my mouth, he whirled around on the bed, settling between my thighs. The next thing I knew, my legs were on his shoulder, and his palms were holding my cheeks apart. He was looking at my most private place like it was a steak or something. It made me blush, because no one had ever looked at me there before. Not for the length of time or with the level of intensity Kent had in his eyes.

Slowly, he moved closer, then he licked a stripe up my crack, making me cry out to the point I had to put my hand over my mouth. He gave me a stern look and mumbled for me to hush, but it was difficult. Every dream I'd ever dreamed was coming true, and it had me arching off the bed, unable to control myself.

The sounds that left me were raw and animalistic. Each time his tongue dragged across my hole, it felt like I was coming undone from the inside out.

His tongue probed at my hole until it eventually pushed past the ring of muscle, making me cry out in pleasure. He reached up and placed a hand over my mouth.

"Someone's going to hear. Baby, you've got to be quiet."

"Sorry," I whispered, feeling a little breathless. "You just feel so good. I didn't know it was supposed to feel this good."

A smirk quirked in the corner of his mouth. "Wait until I'm inside you. The toy feels really good when I play with it, so I'm pretty sure I can make you feel good, too."

I nodded. "Okay. Yeah, Kent. Make me feel good." He looks around the room, but I'm not sure what he's looking for. "What's wrong?"

"Do you have anything we can use for lube?"

I cocked an eyebrow. "Lube? For what?"

He rolled his eyes. "For my dick. It's going to be inside you, and lube will help. I use a lot of it with my toy. I know your momma wouldn't let you have actual lube, but maybe if you've got some lotion or something?"

I hopped off the bed and rushed to grab the bottle of lotion off my dresser. Normally, I wore it because it smelled good, and Momma refused to let me buy cologne, claiming it was a gateway drug to promiscuity, but I didn't think there was anything wrong with wanting to smell good.

When I returned, I held the lotion out for him, and he took it, staring at the bottle. "It's not ideal, but it'll do in a pinch. I'll make sure to keep some lube in my overnight bag, so we're covered next time." He squirted a dollop in his palm, then coated his finger and pressed it against my hole. "Deep breath, Gray. Here I come."

I closed my eyes and waited for him to breach my entrance, and when he did, it made my insides burn. It wasn't painful, just a bit uncomfortable, but nothing I couldn't manage. For the next five minutes, he slid in and out, occasionally adding another finger to stretch me wider. The whole time he was working me open, his eyes never left mine.

"I love you," he whispered, adding a third finger. "I promise, I'm going to be as gentle as I can. If it hurts too much, just tell me. We can change positions. Or just go back to sucking each other."

"It's okay. I'm ready. I've been ready for it, Half-pint," I said.

He swallowed thickly, his eyes dipping down my body, drinking in the sight of me. Wanting to give him a show, I wrapped my hand around my shaft and slowly stroked it. "I think about you when I do this. Every night, I always picture you."

His smile widened. "Yeah?"

"Every night," I confirmed. "Go on. I'm ready."

He lowered my legs and repositioned us, then applied pressure as he pushed forward, making me cry out. It felt like I was being torn in two, but I knew I couldn't give up. Not if it meant making Kent happy. I leaned forward and claimed him with a kiss, hoping the distraction of his tongue tangling with mine might dull some of the pain. To an extent, it did, but not completely. The pressure was still there. It still burned something awful, but it also felt like I was giving part of myself to him. A part that had always been Kent's. He slowly entered me, his tongue tearing through my mouth with abandon. I tried to keep my voice down, but wasn't successful in the slightest. How could I be quiet when every dream I'd ever had was coming true?

Once he was fully enveloped, he stared at the place we were connected and grinned a goofy grin. "I'm inside you, Gray."

"I know," I said, nodding. "Feels good."

"You're sure?"

"Yeah. Keep going, Half-pint. Please?"

Slowly, he pulled out until only the head was still inside. He bit his lip as he slid back inside. Once he was buried to the hilt, he swatted my hand away from my erection and grabbed on, slowly stroking me in time with each of his thrusts. I felt fuller than I ever had, like I was stretched to my limit. He sawed in and out of me with short, quick thrusts, and I found they felt a lot less painful than the long thrusts he started out with.

It didn't take us long until we were both panting and moaning like the women in those movies Trevor used to make me watch with him. Eventually, Kent had to put his hand over my mouth to keep me quiet, but it didn't help all that much.

"I'm close," he said, his breathing ragged. "Can I come inside you?"

I nodded emphatically, rocking my hips to meet each of his thrusts. It was starting to feel incredible, and he kept hitting this spot that had me seeing stars.

"Please, Kent. Mark me. Make me yours."

The words were like the kiss of life, launching him into a series of jackhammer-like moves, repeatedly nailing that magic button inside me. The bed was squeaking so loud, it was a wonder we hadn't woken my mother down the hall. Thankfully, when she took her sleeping pills, she was usually dead to the world.

"I'm going to come," he whined, his movements faster, the grip he had on my cock tightening. "Come with me, baby."

I rolled my hips, grinding into his fist as I squeezed and released my entrance on an endless loop, desperate to provide Kent with the same pleasure he was providing me. His eyes rolled back in his head, his body went stiff, as my orgasm crashed over me, warmth spread inside me. We were coming together, just like he'd asked.

When it was done—as we laid there in those fleeting seconds and months and minutes—I could see our future so clearly. I'd sing. He'd sit behind a desk. I'd have dinner hot and ready for him the second he walked in the door. His stomach would probably hate me for it, because I could hardly make macaroni without burning it, but he'd kiss me anyway, telling me it tasted perfect. We'd get ourselves a nice little house, maybe on the water so it felt like home. I'd love him.

I was going to love him for the rest of my life.

The door burst open, and it felt like every drop of comfort evaporated around us. Like someone turned twenty space heaters on high and aimed them in our direction. Kent was still on top of me, riding out the last wave of his orgasm. When I turned toward the door, my heart sank in my chest. Trevor and two of his buddies were standing there, staring on in horror.

I grabbed the blanket, trying to shield Kent's naked body from them, but staring at Trevor, the second our eyes connected, I knew it was pointless.

He looked like he wanted to kill Kent.

Trevor lunged.

He gave me no chance to react. No time to pull Kent under my body to protect him. To keep him safe, the way I swore I would. Kent's eyes were on mine, the fear clear in them. I reached for him, but he was already being pulled away from me. Jumping up to my knees, I hobbled to the end of the bed, trying to get to them. I sucked in a sharp breath when Trevor landed his first hit.

And then Kent was groaning. Curling up into a tiny, fragile ball. He writhed on the floor in pain, calling out to me.

"Gray!" Kent was screaming for me. Pleading for me to help. I stood up and rushed toward Trevor, but Tommy caught me first, clotheslining me with his arm as I tried to run past. His arm smashed against my throat, knocking the wind out of me, and I fell to my knees unable to breathe.

"Don't fucking touch him!" Kent's voice was like a sonic boom. An explosion of rage so powerful, it sent a chill through me. He jolted up and tried to get to me. Our eyes locked, and the look he gave me wasn't one of fear, it was pure, undeniable passion. "Two-liter, I—"

"I know. I know, Kent."

Then Trevor kneed Kent's stomach so hard, he doubled over, hugging his tummy. Kyle stood in the doorway looking like a deer in headlights. His eyes were open as wide as they'd go, and he just stood there watching it all unfold. Trevor hollered at him to help grab Kent, but he didn't budge.

"Kyle!" I shouted, hoping I might be able to appeal to his good nature. "You gotta help us."

Trevor whipped his head in Kyle's direction, flashing him a terrifying glare. "Get your ass in here." Kyle shook his head and slowly backed away, but my brother wasn't having it. Slamming Kent to the floor, he lunged for Kyle, and I made my move. I knew if I could just get to Kent—if I could get hold of his hand—I could drag him down to my mother's room. Trevor wouldn't touch him there. He wouldn't risk my mother's wrath. Tommy was on me when I lunged, jumping in front of me to block my path to Kent. I dove to the ground, sailing past his leg and landing beside Kent.

Oh, God. Kent.

His eye was already turning an awful shade of purple, and I couldn't bring myself to look at him. I knew this was my fault. Every hit, every kick. It was down to me and my loud mouth. I knew I'd been moaning too loud when we were in bed together, and knowing all of this was because I couldn't keep my big mouth shut felt like slashes to my skin. Sucker-punches to my heart. Ice in my veins. It was all my fault.

"Baby," I whispered, cupping his cheek with my hand. "We have to get out of here. Come on."

"He'll hurt you," he whispered. "I can take it. It's okay. I don't want you getting—" Kent screamed as Tommy's foot connected with the side of his face, and I saw red. I lunged up, reaching for the picture of me and Kent on my bedside table. While Tommy was busy attacking him, I smashed the frame over his head. Tommy let out a cry and covered his head as blood dripped down his forehead, creating little red lines down his fingers. As he stumbled back, I grabbed Kent's wrist and pulled, launching him up off the floor. We made it through the door and took a left toward the stairwell, but Trevor and Kyle were standing in front of it, Trevor still screaming at him. I pulled Kent to my right and ran to Momma's bedroom and twisted the knob.

Locked.

Why the hell was it locked? Momma normally didn't even shut it, just left it cracked in case we needed her. I banged on the door, desperate to get her attention. "Momma! Momma, please!"

The next sound I heard was Kent crying out. I turned to my left and watched in horror as Trevor's fist slammed into his stomach. Tommy stumbled out of my room, still holding his head. Our eyes connected, and I could tell that if he had his way, in that moment, he would have killed me.

"Fucking piece of shit faggot," he hissed at me. I didn't pay him any attention, because he wasn't who I was worried about. Trevor was dragging Kent to the staircase as I continued banging on Momma's door.

Why the hell wasn't she answering? The hallway was filled with echoing screams that crashed off the walls and collided into each other, and she'd slept right through them. Realizing banging on her door wasn't going to get me anywhere, I set my aim on Trevor. I rushed past Tommy, chasing after my brother as he dragged Kent back into my bedroom.

"You think you can fuck my brother and walk out of here? Are you really that fucking stupid, Kent Fox?"

"Just let me go, Trevor!" he yelled back, his voice stronger than it had any right to be. When I turned the corner into my bedroom, Kent was standing up, facing my brother. He wasn't backing down. He wasn't letting Trevor see him as weak or broken.

"I'll tell you what," Trevor said, his nostrils flaring. "I'll let you go, but I want you to end it. Tell Grayson he's dead to you. That you're never going to speak to him again. If you do that, I'll let you walk out of here right now." Kent's eyebrows drew together, and he turned to me, tears pooling in his eyes.

He could have lied. That's all he had to do. He could tell me that he never loved me, and that tonight had been a mistake. He'd know I wouldn't believe it. Then, once Daddy got home, he'd fix it. He could talk sense into Trevor.

"Say it," I whispered. I nodded at Kent, mouthing that it was okay. Silently pleading for him to just say the words. Begging Kent to break my heart before Trevor broke his neck. "Say it, Half-pint. Please?"

He sniffled, his bottom lip wedged between his teeth as he bit down. Kent's hands were shaking, and God, I wanted to hold him and tell him everything was gonna be okay. That we'd survive this, and we could still be together. We might not be able to talk until Trevor left for college, but what was a few more months when we had our entire lives ahead of us?

Kent smiled at me. It was big and bright and so fucking beautiful I almost couldn't stand it. It was one for the record books. One that filled my heart with pride. Then he shook his head.

My heart cracked in my chest. I couldn't breathe.

"Say it. Dammit, Kent, say it!"

He walked toward me, his head held high. With his hand pressed against my steadily breaking heart, he said, "I've loved you, Gray Collins, from the second I looked up and saw you in that desk next to me, I fucking loved you." Kent's smile widened even more, his eyes never leaving mine. "You can go fuck yourself, Trevor."

Trevor nodded, and then he made his way toward us. Hs reared back his hand and smacked Kent in the back of the head with his palm, sending him crashing to the floor. I cried out for him, tears scalding like little drops of acid tore into my flesh, leaving me raw and exposed. He grabbed Kent by the neck and jerked him to his feet. As Trevor turned toward the door, dragging the only person who made a bit of sense in this world to me behind, our eyes connected.

"I love you, Gray. I love you so—"

Trevor slammed him into the doorframe, and Kent let out a wail that ripped my heart to shreds.

"Where are you taking him? Trevor, where the hell are you taking him?" My voice was broken, my throat raw like it was filled with gravel. I tried to follow after them, making it to the bedroom door before Trevor turned around and glared at me. The look he was giving me was one I'd never seen before. His pupils were dilated so wide, it looked like his entire eyes were black. He took a step forward, and then he slammed his fist into my stomach, dropping me to my knees.

"You sit your ass down and wait here until I come back. So help me, Grayson, if you follow us, I'll fucking kill him." Trevor eyed me up and down, the disgust clear on his face. "You make me sick. The things he was doing—what you were allowing him to do to you. It's demonic. You stay right here, and you beg God for forgiveness. When I get back, we're gonna have a nice, long talk."

"Trev, please! Don't hurt him. He didn't do anything I didn't ask him to. I wanted it. Probably more than he did."

He flinched, tensing up like the words stung him. "Fucking filth. That's what this is. I've seen the way he looks at you, and it ain't right. You stay on your knees, and you pray. You understand me?"

"You won't hurt him?"

He reached over, shoving me by the shoulders until I fell back against the floorboards, banging my head against the side of the bed as I fell. "I will if you don't do what the hell I just told you to. I'm not playing, Gray. You sit right there, and you think about what the hell you've done. If you step foot outside of this room, I'll kill him in front of you. I'll make it hurt."

I couldn't choke back the sob that was climbing up my throat. It was panic and pure terror. Kent needed me right then. He might not have known it. He might have thought I was letting them take him because I was a coward—and maybe I was. But if that's what it took to keep him safe—to keep him alive—what choice did I have?

I took a deep breath, and I nodded.

Trevor turned to walk away, peering over his shoulder at me one last time before pulling the door shut behind him.

My head was in a fog. It almost felt like it did the night Kent blew that smoke in my face. I was dizzy and disoriented, lying in a naked heap on my bedroom floor. My head was throbbing from where I'd gotten hit, but I didn't worry about that. I couldn't worry about it. They could be taking Kent anywhere, doing God knows what to him.

Kent's clothes were still resting where he left them. I saw his shirt on my dresser. His underwear hung from my bedpost, and his jeans were by my door. Trevor didn't even let him take his shoes. His feet were going to get hurt from the gravel in the driveway.

I fell to my knees, staring out the window and into the sky. "Please," I pleaded with Him. "Please, don't let them hurt him. I won't touch him again. I won't love him anymore if that's what it takes. You just gotta help him. I won't ever talk to him again, but please, just let him be okay."

Time ran on its own wavelength for a while. Seconds morphed to days which were divided into minutes and months. Alone in my bedroom without the familiarity of God, without Kent's hopeful heart, was torture. Images flashed in my mind of the things they might be doing to him.

I could try to wake Momma again, but when she took her sleeping pill it took an act of God to get her to stir. And even then, sometimes that wasn't enough. A couple of years before we moved to Texas, a twister tore through Little Rock. It touched down a few miles from our house and quickly made its way toward us. Trevor tried to shake Momma awake, but she slept right through it. Even when he dragged her from her bed to the bathroom and laid her in the bathtub. Daddy had been at work, and it was just the three of us there. While Trevor hauled my mattress into the bathroom, I stood frozen in place, unable to move. I watched through the living room window as swing sets and lawn mowers took flight. It was like watching that *Wizard of Oz* movie. I watched as it ripped my friend Carrie's bicycle out of her lawn and into its vortex.

It's funny, the places your mind goes when the reality is too scary to process. As her pink bike was lifted from the ground, I imagined what it must be like to ride the bike into the eye of the storm. Would it hurt to peddle your way through a cyclone? Would the sheer force of it all tear the breath from your body? Cause that's how this felt. Sitting alone in a room that seemed so full of promise half an hour back, that's exactly what it felt like when they tore Kent away from me. My brother jerked the future I'd planned out of reality with that first punch to his gut. The second they came into my bedroom, I knew we were over. Trevor would never let us be happy. The rage in his eyes, and then the strength of his push, had brought me to my knees.

The front door opened and closed. I tucked myself into a ball in my closet, praying it was Kent coming to find me. In my prayer, he would tell me he fought them off one by one before talking them down. He'd say he made them see the light.

"You can't see him again. You get that, right?"

With my head buried in the crook of my elbow, I hadn't even heard him approach. Hadn't heard the door open or his heavy footsteps against the wooden floorboards.

"Is he okay?" It was the only question that mattered. The only prayer I needed to have been answered.

"He's alive," he said before kneeling in front of me. "I let him live because you begged me to. The things he was doing to you, Grayson ... Jesus. It's fucked.

It ain't natural. All of that, every bit of this filth, it ends tonight. Do you understand me?"

I didn't respond. I couldn't make my mouth work. Instead, I sat there, my entire body shaking, sobbing as Trevor explained the dream I'd dreamt of me and Kent side by side for the rest of our lives was gone. Beaten out of possibility with every punch they threw.

"You so much as look at him, and I'll drag his ass back out to the lake and finish it."

I gasped.

The lake. Our lake. The one I found just for us. That hurt almost as much as losing him. The lake was ours. Our hidden oasis where we could simply exist. Where there was no cruelty. No judgment. Not a single bit of shame sent our way by people who didn't understand the depth of our friendship. The lingering hugs. The endless affection. That lake was ours, and in less than an hour, Trevor took that from us. He took it from him.

Trevor was at my bedroom door when I finally managed to make my voice work. "What did you do to him?"

Trevor snickered. It felt like he was getting off on this. Like he used my fear as some sort of war tactic to guarantee his victory.

"Poured gas on him and struck a few matches to scare him."

I shoved my face into my arms and wailed. Vicious, broken, choppy sounds that echoed across the walls. I cried for many things at that moment. For the loss of Kent. The loss of our future. The fear he must have felt every time Trevor struck a match. Mainly, I cried to God.

"I hate you. I hate you with everything I've got in me."

His breath was hot against my skin. I hadn't even noticed when he knelt beside me. "Hate me all you want. If that's what it takes to keep you out of Hell, I'll take it. I know it hurts, but I'm doing this for you. Everything I did tonight was for you. Hate me all you want. I love you enough to let you."

"Screw you." I pressed my face into my knees and whimpered; tiny, pathetic little sounds. "Screw you, screw you, screw you!"

"You know I'm right. That's why you're fighting it so hard. You know what the Bible says about it, Gray. You know."

"I'll tell Daddy," I threatened, still unable to look him in the eyes.

He clutched my chin in his hand and jerked my face toward him until our eyes met. "I wasn't playing. One word. To Momma, to Daddy, to anyone. I'll kill him. It ends tonight. When you go to school Monday, you're moving desks to right beside Sister Thorpe. Lunchtime, you sit at your desk. You can forget about breaks, too. Unless you have to piss, you keep your ass in that damn chair, and you do your schoolwork. I'll come by to check. Kyle and Tommy will keep tabs. If you so much as look at him, I'll do it. I swear to God, I will."

He would. As I stared into the dark, demonic eyes glaring back at me, I didn't have a shred of doubt that he'd kill Kent.

"I hate you."

"Like I said, I'll take that. For now, I want you to get your ass in that bed and go to sleep. You don't leave this room until I'm awake. Understood?"

"Screw you."

He pulled his arm back and slapped me across the face. "Understood?"

"Y-yeah. Yeah, I get it. Just go."

Chapter Seven

I ached for him. Knowing how he felt for me, witnessing my brother dragging him away. Every fiber of my being screamed for me to go to him. To wrap him in my arms and tell him he was safe. If I did that—if I gave into those urges—Trevor would kill him. The hate in his eyes when he told me what he did to Kent; I don't know if I've ever seen that much rage in one person.

I tried to reconcile it all with God. For the last three days I'd done little more than that. But God must've been away from the phone, because as hard as I tried, I couldn't see him as anything other than a monster.

The classroom door opened, and I didn't have to turn around to know it was Kent. A chill ran down my spine as his footsteps approached from behind me.

You can do this.

It took everything in me not to launch out of my chair and wrap him up in my arms.

You have to do this.

His chair groaned its displeasure when he sat down. I waited to hear the wheels sliding against the floor tiles, but they didn't. The dividers between our desks were like a shield, warding off the hurt his beautiful face would shoot through me.

The longer we sat silently, his eyes burning holes in my back and invading my senses, the heavier my heart weighed in my chest. I wanted him to turn around and face his desk. I needed him to let go of this thing between us. If Trevor kept his word and came to school to check on me and saw I was talking to Kent, he would kill him.

I wanted to look at Kent so badly. To tell him I was still there and that I still loved him with everything I had in me, but our love wasn't worth him losing his life. Letting him go would hurt him, but he'd be better off in the long run. Kent Fox was the love of my life, and if breaking his heart meant he would still have a heart to break, it would be worth it. His hurt. My hurt. All of our hurt combined. None of it was worth dying over.

I would die a death of sorts. The death of possibility. The death of a life filled with purpose. I'd marry a girl I could never truly love, and Kent would go on without me. He would go on to live a big, beautiful life full of love and sass and passion. He could be open and honest about his sexuality in a way I never could. It would be a life he could be proud of.

It just couldn't be with me.

I could never have that. Trevor made sure I knew as much when he came back that night.

"Gray." His voice hitched, cracking and shattering as he spoke. "Two-liter, please..."

What was I supposed to say to that? How the heck was I supposed to respond? I couldn't tell him he meant nothing to me, because those words ... Those nasty, awful, terrible words would break us both. My only option was avoidance. The sooner I broke his heart, the sooner he could heal it, and Kent Fox deserved to be whole. He deserved everything. He *was* everything.

I couldn't sit next to him and listen to him hurting, knowing I was the reason for it. He would hate me for it. He'd probably never forgive me for abandoning him when he needed me the most, but I'd made a promise. To Trevor and to God. Psalm 51 said *the sacrifices of God are a broken spirit*. Is this what he meant? *A broken and contrite heart, O God, thou wilt not despise.* My heart was both. Broken, like the shattered dreams that fell like tears around me. Contrite, full of remorse; not for sin, but for breaking a man who didn't deserve to be broken. To protect his heart, I had to sacrifice my own. I owed him that much.

I grabbed my workbooks and the cup with my pens and pencils. The picture of Kent and me after Momma and I gave him Abe was pinned to the desk.

Another relic of the love story that never got the chance to be told. I took it down and shoved it in my pocket.

I love you.

"Gray?"

I'd never questioned God before, but sitting there—with Kent so close I could have reached out and touched him—I didn't know what type of a god would put someone through that much pain. And for what? Because a book spread hate when it was meant to inspire love?

God and I weren't on speaking terms at the moment.

"Baby, please. Just look at me." Kent grabbed my wrist as I walked past, his touch like tiny twinges of electricity shooting through my bloodstream.

I couldn't. He had to know that. He'd seen Trevor's rage firsthand.

Don't hate me.

I shrugged his hand off of me without looking back at him and walked across the room to Sister Thorpe's desk. I peeked over my shoulder, needing to see him. Needing to bear witness to the damage left in my wake.

Don't regret me.

Kent was turned around in his seat, facing the front of his cubicle. I watched him longer than I should have—longer than I had any right to.

Please don't forget me.

Please?

"Gray? Sugar, did you need something?" Sister Thorpe's voice was meek; always quiet, calm, and full of care. She stared at my face like she was studying scripture, reaching each line and trying to uncover its teachings.

"Sweetie, what's wrong?" She reached for me, taking my hand and squeezing gently. I shook my head, and then I pulled my hand away. "Are you feeling sick? Your skin's whiter than snow." She stood up and walked around her desk toward me. Behind me, classmates chuckled at each other's jokes. Guys talked about the girls they wanted to ask out. Girls talked about what they would wear to Sunday service. Everyone's life went on like this was a normal day. Like the very fabric of reality hadn't shattered around me two nights before. Like God hadn't abandoned them when they needed Him most.

"He's fine," Tommy said. My entire body tensed. I hadn't even heard him come in. "He was going to ask if it's okay if he moves to the desk next to mine. I already talked to Kyle, he said he'd switch seats with Gray if you'd let him."

I jerked my head toward Tommy and gaped at him. That wasn't part of the plan. Kent had already suffered enough. He didn't need his attacker sitting next to him every day. I turned back toward the classroom, searching out for someone. For anyone.

Her eyes met mine, and I could finally breathe again.

Kate stood up and walked toward us, her eyes never leaving mine. When she reached me, she grabbed my hand and pulled me toward the door. I didn't look back at Tommy. I already knew that he was glaring at me with threats and revulsion in his eyes.

"We'll be back in a second. I just need to talk to Gray really quick, Sister Thorpe."

Sister Thorpe eyed me curiously, and there was a knowingness in her gaze. I didn't know how much she'd caught onto, but it must have been enough to know I needed a second.

"Take your seat, Tommy. You've got two weeks' worth of work left in your science book. Get started on that, and we'll talk about the desk situation when they get back."

Kate didn't wait for Tommy to respond, she just pulled me out of the classroom, down the hallway, and into the breakroom. I thought we were going to stop there, but she kept walking until we were out the door and in the backyard. We walked to the swing set, and she sat in the one on the left before motioning for me to join her. I obliged, my knees popping as I lowered myself into the swing. They'd been doing that a lot since Saturday night. During the chaos, someone must have kicked them, because they'd been aching something awful ever since. When I told Momma I was worried I'd sprained them somehow, she just looked at me like I was stupid.

She'd done that a few times since Sunday morning. I knew Trevor hadn't told her anything, but the looks she'd give me at church, right up until bedtime—there was a knowingness in her eyes, just like Sister Thorpe. I worried maybe God had come to each of them and told them all the horrible, blasphemous things I said to him while I waited for Trevor to come back home from the lake.

"Gray?" Kate practically shouted at me.

I startled. "What?"

"I've been saying your name for a minute straight. What the heck is going on? You look like death warmed over." I couldn't look at her. If I would have just let them keep on dating, if I hadn't made Kent break up with her and come back to my bedroom, I'd be sitting beside him right then, not a single care in the world. "Something's going on. Kent's face is all banged up and you look like someone just killed your dog." I bit my lip to keep myself from crying. "Listen, I know we've never been that close, but I can tell something's wrong. If you want to talk about it, I'm here. Just me and you, no one else has to know."

"I can't," I choked out. I could feel the walls I'd built up around my heart starting to crumble, and I knew one wrong word would send them falling to the ground, leaving us in a dusty downfall of broken-hearted admissions. Words I could never unsay. She and Kent were together ... intimately. So she must have felt something for him. She must have liked him enough to jerk him off at the lake. I didn't want her going back in and telling everyone. That would just add insult to injury to my Half-pint, and I couldn't hurt him anymore.

She nodded. "Okay. I won't pry." She held her hand out, and I turned and balked at her. I'd been nothing but nasty to her, and there she was, trying to ease my hurt as much as she could. I didn't deserve it. Not after the nasty, horrible things I said about her. Not after forcing Kent to hurt her heart, even if mine had been hurt just as hard.

I reached for her, weaving my fingers with her, hands dangling between our swings, and I broke. Out there, on that rickety old swing set, I shattered. Tears fell like shards of glass from a crumbling building.

"I've got a great-uncle. Even though I never met him, my great-aunt Dottie tells me about him sometimes. I think you two would have gotten along well," she said. "He died before I was born. Dottie doesn't talk about him too much. I can tell it hurts her to think about him, but sometimes you have to walk through the hurt to reach a peaceful heart. That's what my father says, at least." She squeezed my hand harder. "He was gay."

I sucked in a sharp breath; the air felt like jagged ice inside my lungs. Like it was ripping away the lining until I was nothing more than slivers of tissue, hanging on by a wing and a prayer.

"Something happened to him. Someone told the wrong person. He died when he was just a kid." She turned and stared at me, but I still couldn't meet her gaze. "I know what the Bible says, but I also know there isn't anything wrong with love. The heart wants what it wants, and no book is going to change my mind about it." She paused, taking in a breath before squeezing my hand again. "You look me in the eyes, Gray Collins." I whipped my head in her direction. "There is nothing wrong with the way you feel about him. You hear me? Nothing at all."

She knew. Oh, God. She knew, and she must have known for a while. Did that mean she knew I asked him to break up with her? Had she known I'd tried to trick him into leaving her by claiming she was cheating? She knew, and she held all the power in the world. She could tell everyone just to spite me.

"He never looked at me the way he looks at you. Sometimes I would catch him staring at you, just lost in his own head for minutes on end. I thought maybe he might like guys and girls, but that wasn't the case. I found out for sure on Saturday night. Kent called me at two in the morning, sobbing into the phone. He said something happened, and that he couldn't see me anymore. He must have apologized a hundred times. I didn't know he'd gotten hurt until he came to class this morning."

He called her. After everything, he still called her to end things. Did he do it for me? Was he still hoping we could be together? Could we still be together?

"Kate, you g-gotta get someone else to take my old seat. Kyle can't sit there, it'll—" I choked out another cry, and Kate was in front of me in a split second, wrapping her arms around me and holding me tight. "He sh-shouldn't h-have to sit next to him, it'll break him. You gotta—"

"Hey!" she said, full of force. "I've got this. I've got him, you don't have to beg. Of course, I'll find someone else to sit there."

"He's been through so much, he doesn't deserve—"

"I have this," she repeated, punching out each of the words.

***

June 2003

Two months passed since Trevor hurt him. Two months spent sitting in the same room with only space and stillness separating us. Trevor was true to his word. Tommy followed me like a shadow, clinging to my every move—my every glance—like he owned me.

I guess he did, in a way. I guess all three of them did.

Kent stopped trying to talk to me about a week after it all happened. Every plea, every unacknowledged greeting felt like I was kicking him the same way those boys did. Like I was the one dousing him in gasoline and striking matches to scare him off.

My world came tumbling down the day after graduation. I was sitting at the table with Momma and Trevor, talking about traveling around to different churches where I could sing for congregations. She'd never supported my passion before, but it was like there was a heavy weight on her, and allowing me this one thing somehow alleviated the pressure.

I picked at my scrambled eggs with disinterest as Trevor droned on about attending community college in the fall. Momma cleared her throat, cutting him off.

"I talked to Mrs. Fox at the Pick-n-Save yesterday."

I jerked my head up and stared at her. She hadn't mentioned any of the Fox family since that night. I'd assumed she could tell the subject hurt too much and she was trying to keep my heart safe by not prying. But I wanted her to pry. I wanted her to mention Kent. Did Sister Fox tell her Kent got hurt? If she knew, then she could override Trevor. Momma could make it all better by telling me to go to Kent. Trevor wouldn't call me out in front of her. If he did, it meant telling her everything else that happened in my room.

"She said Kent's leaving West Clark. He's heading out to Dallas to chase his dreams."

My heart sank.

He couldn't. Kent didn't have any dreams outside the city. I was his dream. He told me so.

"Good riddance," Trevor said, his voice heavy with disgust. I wanted to take my butter knife and plunge it into his hand, but hearing about Kent—getting to talk about him again—that meant more to me than making Trevor hurt like I was hurting.

"Dallas? What's he going to do in Dallas? He doesn't know anyone out there. He doesn't know anyone outside of West Clark besides his Aunt Jeanie, and she lives in Tyler."

Momma shrugged. "I couldn't tell you. Caterina just said he was leaving. Seemed torn up about it, but I guess that's natural." She stared at me with a smile. "God knows I'd be beside myself if either of you left." Her eyes narrowed slightly, but her smile remained locked in place. "I don't think I'd survive if you moved away, baby. I'm just so thankful I raised you to know where home is. That it's with your family. You do know that, right?"

I didn't know what the heck she was getting at, I just knew Kent was leaving. He was leaving West Clark. He was leaving me.

"When is he moving?"

She stared down at her watch, her hand shaking slightly. "His bus should be leaving right about ..." She paused, her head nodding with each tick of her watch. "Now."

No. He couldn't. He wouldn't.

Kent would never leave without telling me goodbye. I knew that. I knew it deep down in the darkest, loneliest corners of my heart. Even if he had a bus ticket, he would wait for me. Wait for me to come and tell him goodbye.

He would wait for me to join him on his new journey. Together. Always.

It was less of a thought and more of an epiphany. If I could just make it to him in time, I could go with him. We would lose our families, but we'd have each other. I just had to get to him.

"I have to use the bathroom." I launched up from my chair like a rocket shooting toward the sky. Because that's what I was doing, wasn't it? Launching out of West Clark, toward a new world, full of love and endless possibility.

I bolted up the stairs, ignoring Trevor's heavy footsteps behind me. I ran into my room and grabbed my backpack without even trying to close my door.

I was an adult. An eighteen-year-old man who didn't have to live by any of their rules anymore. Trevor was welcome to try to stop me. He could even threaten to out me to our parents. It didn't matter anymore. None of them mattered.

"I know what you're thinking of doing, and I won't let it happen, Grayson," Trevor said behind me.

"Screw you." I emptied my backpack onto the bed and ran toward my dresser, pulling out enough clothes to get me by.

"I told you what would happen if you talked to him again. I told you what I'd do to him. If you do it, I'll set that faggot's ass on fire and make you watch him burn."

"Set yourself on fire. How about that?" I dumped my piggy bank into the backpack and zipped it closed. When I turned around, Trevor was blocking the door.

"I'm not letting you do this. There's no use anyway, he's already gone."

"I'm not letting him leave. I don't care if I have to beg him, he's going back home, and you're going to leave him alone."

He snorted. "Home? Are you an idiot? He ain't got a home. He ain't chasing his dreams, dipshit. His dad kicked his queer ass out the second he turned eighteen. He knows his son's a faggot."

I shook my head. "Kent wouldn't tell him. He wouldn't."

He shrugged. "I did." My heart slammed in my chest. "Is that what you want? Do you want Momma and Daddy to find out about you, too? Don't think I won't tell them."

I hated him. Probably more than I'd ever hated anyone. He was nothing more than a bully who got off on harassing smaller kids, just because he could. That's all he would ever be. He'd go to community college, get a job managing a gas station or a fast-food restaurant, and that's all he'd ever be. He'd hoard hatred like ammunition he could use to ward off his feelings of failure. To make himself feel better than others. That was fine. He was welcome to do so.

But I wouldn't. I refused to become him. To be stuck here with him.

Me and Kent, we might struggle for a while—we might end up sleeping on the streets until we found jobs—but we would live. We would have each other. That's something Trevor could never have. He might make a decent-enough living as a manager or something, but he'd never have what Kent and I did. He needed to have a heart to fall in love, and his was charred and blackened like it had been left on the grill too long. That's what happens when you invite hate in. It burns away at you, leaving nothing but ash in its wake.

"If you don't get the hell out of my way, I'm calling the police. I'm eighteen, you don't get to boss me around no more, Trevor. This is my life, not yours. For fuck's sake!"

He reared back his hand and slapped me. "Watch your mouth!"

Momma gasped.

She must have been standing outside the door. I didn't know how long she'd been there or how much she'd heard, but I didn't care one way or the other.

"You're a bully, Trev. You're a bully and a jerk, and I hope one day someone does to you what you've done to me. What you've done to him. And when it happens"—I took a step forward, driving my finger into his chest as hard as I could—"I hope it breaks you. I hope it eats away at you so bad that even God can't help you heal. And when you ask Him for help—when you cry out to Him in the middle of the night—I pray He doesn't answer. I pray He abandons you, because that's what you deserve."

"Steady now, you're saying stuff you're not going to be able to take back—"

"I don't want to take it back. I want you to know exactly what you are to me. You're a coward, Trevor. A coward and a bigot, and even God can't save you from what you've done. So, you can get out of my way, and then you can go straight to Hell." I shoved my palms into his chest so hard that he stumbled backward, crashing into the hallway wall. When I walked out of the bedroom, Momma's face was white as a ghost.

"Grayson," she said, her voice hardly even a whisper. "You can't ..."

"I love you," I said, pulling her in for a hug. "I love you more than the whole world, but I'm not staying here while Kent's out there without anyone. He's ..." I choked back the sob demanding release. There would be time enough for tears when this was over. "He's no good on his own. He needs somebody."

In that moment, I thought of finally saying it. I was almost home free, and I had nothing to lose. I could have just opened my mouth and blurted out that I was gay, and that I was going to spend the rest of my life with Kent Fox, but there was still that small twinge inside. The little string of doubt hiding in my heart.

What if he's already gone? What if he's gone and doesn't want you anymore? What are you going to do then?

"What the hell is all this racket about?" My father's voice rang out from down the hall. "For the love of God, I've been up all night trying to deliver a damn calf, and the second I manage to get a little shut-eye, you all lose your minds."

His eyes were half-lidded with sleep as he made his way to us. When he spotted the backpack in my hand, he cocked an eyebrow at me. "I thought school ended last week."

"It did," I answered, pushing past Momma. I made it into the hallway, but Daddy was standing in front of the stairs, blocking my path to freedom.

"Then where in the world are you going, buddy?" He cocked a smile at me. "Don't tell me, you and Kent are heading out to the lake. I knew you'd be back on speaking terms soon enough."

He didn't know Kent was leaving town? Why wouldn't Momma tell him?

"His parents kicked him out. He's getting on a bus and heading for Dallas." Tears welled in my eyes, but I didn't bother wiping them away.

Dad's jaw went slack, his mouth hanging open. "Why the hell would Joel and Cat kick him out?"

I shot a glare at Trevor. "Because they found out he's gay."

Trevor and Momma's gazes dropped to the floor, but Daddy's stayed locked on me. The muscles in his jaw flexed, and his hands were fisted at his sides. For a second, I thought he was going to forbid me from ever seeing him again.

"Grayson," he said, taking in a deep breath when he was done. "Go." My heart stalled in my chest. I knew it. He was kicking me out. Just like Kent's daddy.

"Marty," Momma whispered, but he didn't pay her any mind. He was too busy searching my face for something hidden beneath the surface. He must have sensed something was off, because he reached out and squeezed my shoulder.

"Go to the bus station, son. Don't let him get on that bus. If he's not there, come home and wait by the phone." He turned around and headed back to his room. I trailed behind, not sure what he was suggesting. When I made it to their door, he was already sliding on his shoes and grabbing his keys off the end of the dresser. "Get a move on. Those buses run behind, we've still got a chance."

"What are you—Where am I supposed to take him if I find him? His parents kicked him out."

He sighed, rolling his eyes. "Here, son. You bring him here. Kent's family. I'm not having him sleeping on the damn streets."

I couldn't. Trevor would kill him. But I could go with him. If I could make it in time, we could both leave together. It would be like one of those Hallmark movies Ms. Dottie taped for Kent and stealthily slipped his way when Pastor Fox wasn't looking. It would be our happy ending. The beginning of our forever.

"Where are you going?" I asked.

"I'm going to have myself a nice, long talk with Pastor Fox. Now, hurry up. Get down there and bring him home."

I turned and ran down the stairs, past the picture-lined walls showing the story of our family. That family was fractured now, and there wasn't enough glue to put it back together. I raced out the door, toward my pickup truck. Every step I took was a step away from God and toward the man I loved. The man who loved me back. And wasn't that just something? Out of all the men out there, all the hearts he could've chosen, Kent chose mine. It wasn't a particularly unique heart. Just a large mass inside of me that pumped blood with a thumping chorus of *Kent-Kent-Kent*. Still, he chose it. Cherished it. For so long, he kept it safeguarded from all the hurt and ache flung its way. It's like that song, the one I only sang for him. I wasn't what he'd planned on, but maybe I could be what he needed. *Who* he needed me to be.

On the way to my truck, I grabbed a rose from the bush in front of our porch. Something pretty for the man I loved.

Heading down Main Street, I hit every stoplight along the way. I sped down Dudley Avenue, past Bronson's Bakery, making a hard right on North Third Street. The bus station was just past the Pick-n-Save, three intersections down. I skidded to a stop, taking up three parking spaces. I hopped out of my truck, leaving the door wide open, and not even bothering to turn it off.

There were a few cars out front, which gave me hope. Maybe they belonged to family members who'd come to see off their loved ones. Maybe the bus got a flat tire along the way.

Maybe I was just holding out hope for a man who already let me go.

I rushed into the bus station, my eyes darting around frantically, desperate to catch sight of his curly hair. There was a woman by a vending machine, banging the side of her fist against the glass, trying to dislodge a bag of Doritos that had gotten stuck. Across the room, an elderly man was tapping his walking cane against the floor tiles to the beat of the song playing through the speakers.

There were four people in that room. Kent wasn't one of them. I took a seat in the corner of the room, just trying to catch my breath.

He was gone.

Half-pint was gone, and I was never getting him back. Eventually, I got the nerve to ask the man at the counter if he'd seen a boy with curly hair that morning, and he confirmed what I'd been dreading. Kent already hopped on a bus and headed out West.

I had enough money left from helping Dad on the farm to get me to Dallas, but it already felt like I'd lost him. I knew I had to try, though. Heck, with as slow as buses were, I might even make it there before he did. I thought of how romantic it would be for his bus to pull up to the depot, only to be greeted by my smiling face. It would be the first day of the rest of our lives.

Then I saw it.

There, on the counter, in an outgoing mail slot, was a letter with my name front and center. Grayson Collins, it said, and then my address. The man shouted something as I ripped the envelope open, but I couldn't hear a word he said. Once it was open, I unfolded the paper and stared down at the words, my heart shattering. Kent was leaving my life forever, and all he could bring himself to say was, "*I hate you.*"

***

That evening, after I got home, Trevor tried to follow me to my room, but I slammed the door in his face. No matter how many times they banged on my door, I didn't speak to Momma or Daddy. I just couldn't bring myself to open it. I'd never felt as low and lonely as I did that day, and the reality of the situation was starting to sink in.

Half-pint was scared and lonely and all by himself. He wasn't going to have somewhere safe to sleep, and I was hiding in the comfort of my bedroom, not having lost anything. I still had a home. A home which had never felt much like a home at all, occupied by a family that never seemed all too concerned about my feelings.

Two hours later, the doorbell rang. Footsteps clicked and clacked against the hallway's hardwood floors, and a few seconds later there was a knock on my door.

"Leave me alone," I called out, trying to stop my voice from cracking. "I already said I don't want to talk."

"Grayson," a familiar voice called out, her voice soft and broken. Why was Sister Fox at my bedroom door? Did she come to tell Momma and Daddy what Kent and I meant to each other? Would she out me? Was she going to kick my butt for touching her son? "Please open the door."

I swallowed down the lump in my throat and wiped my nose with a tissue from my nightstand, not bothering to dry my cheeks. They'd just get wet again in a minute, so what was the point?

When I opened the door, Sister Fox looked just as hurt as I felt on the inside. Just as emotionally bruised and broken as Kent's face was the night Trevor took him from me. My jaw trembled as another tear dropped down my cheek, and the sight of it triggered something in her, because she steeled her emotions, hardening her face like stone. She'd never looked at me that way. For the past four years, she had been like a second mother to me.

"Don't you dare," she warned. "I just lost my son because of you. Don't even think of crying." Her hands were clenched into fists at her sides, and for a second I worried she was going to drive one of them into my face. I noticed a handprint around her throat like someone tried to choke her or something. Did Momma try to hurt Sister Fox before she made it to my room? "How long was it going on? The sex. How long have you two been intimate?"

I looked away. "Just the once," I whispered, embarrassed. "Just that night."

"Kent wouldn't say a word about it after he got home." She closed her eyes and took a deep breath like she was trying to calm herself down. "Were you at the lake when it happened? Were you a part of it—with the matches?"

I gaped at her. "You think I hurt him? You think I was striking matches with them, too?" I took a step back, repulsed by the accusation. It made me feel physically ill. "He's—" I choked back a sob. "He's my Half-pint. Kent's my everything, I could never hurt him. I would never lay a hand on him."

I took a step back, dizzy and unable to focus. He was gone. He was really gone, and I was alone. The dreams we were dreaming, gone. My one chance at getting out of this town, gone. The love of my life, gone. Trevor would never unhook his claws from me. I saw what he did to Kent. He'd do the same to me if I even thought of coming out. My future was gone.

"You loved him?"

My knees gave way and I fell down on my bed, gripping the side of the mattress and holding on for dear life. "More than anyone." I looked up at her, needing her to know it. "More than God." I wasn't sorry for saying it. Even though I knew it would probably damn my soul to Hell, I would burn endlessly for Kent Fox. "I've always loved him. From the very first day." It felt like my body was caving in on itself. Pressure pressed down on my chest, making it harder to breathe.

"Grayson," she said, her voice softer than before.

I was pleading with my eyes, desperate to make it all stop. To make us go back to that night at the lake, before everything blew up. Maybe I could change it. I could stop him from getting hurt, but God had to let me go back. I would lead him to the old oak tree by the lake instead of taking him back to my room. We would sit and snuggle for hours, laughing about how ridiculous he'd been for thinking I'd be mad at him for being gay, and at how unnecessary his attempt to turn himself straight had been. There was no need to fix himself or hide that part of him, because we weren't born broken.

"You have to go find him. You've got to bring him home. He's no good on his own." I wiped my cheeks with my palms.

"I can't," she said, her face falling into a picture of resignation, her cheeks red with embarrassment. She closed her eyes, and her hands were shaking. I'd never seen her look so small. "Joel won't let me."

"Kent is your son. He needs you. He needs *us*." I stood up, feeling a new spark of hope. "We'll go together. Me and you. Let's go find him and bring him home." I grabbed the kees to my truck off the dresser.

"I can't," she repeated. She sounded so sure of it. It was like she'd been digging a hole for herself, knowing she would never be able to crawl back out.

I turned around and nodded encouragingly. "Sure you can. Come on, there's still time. Daddy says the buses run late, so he's probably not there yet. We'll find him. I know we will—"

"Gray. Sweetie," she whispered, still not looking me in the eyes. She absentmindedly reached up and touched her neck, like she was trying to ease her discomfort. She winced with pain and pulled her hand away. "Joel forbids it."

I felt like I was going to be sick, my stomach clenching and spinning at the same time. "What the hell kind of mother are you?" Her eyes widened in shock, and so did mine. I'd never spoken to anyone like that. I certainly never raised my voice at a lady.

She swallowed, breaking eye contact and looking at the floor. "A heartbroken one," she answered, her voice small and ashamed. She took a deep breath, shaking her head. Again, her hand touched her neck, and yet again, she winced in pain. "A husband's word is final." She sounded like she was reciting scripture she was forced to memorize, the same way Kent and I did when we learned them at school. "Maybe you're right. Maybe I am a terrible mother. I let him down when he needed me." Her jaw worked, back and forth, side to side, tears spilling over.

"So did I," I whispered, so ashamed of myself I couldn't even look her in the eyes. "I know I hurt him and I probably can't ever take that hurt away, but we have to try. If we can just find him, we can find somewhere for him to stay. Miss Dottie would probably let him stay with her. We can't just sit here and—"

"Grayson!" Trevor's voice boomed into the room, echoing off the walls, engulfing every square inch of my bedroom. He was standing in the doorframe, right behind Sister Fox. "Don't say another damn word to her."

Sister Fox's hands were balled into fists, her knuckles white, little red lines stretched across her the creases in her skin. She slowly turned around, and I don't know what look she was giving Trevor, but it couldn't have been good, because he took a step back like he was worried she was going to hit him.

"You ain't welcome here, Caterina." I'd never heard him sound so heartless. He sounded like he wanted to dig a hole to the center of the Earth and toss her into Hell himself. "You're upsetting my brother."

I gaped at him. He was being hateful on my behalf, but I held no hatred for Sister Fox, and I certainly didn't need him to defend me. Sure, I might have said some nasty things to her a few seconds earlier, but Trevor was her son's attacker. He was the whole reason we both lost Kent.

"Don't ever speak to me again," she growled. I'd never heard that level of venom in her voice. She had always had a baby-like tone to her voice, but every trace of that softness was gone. "You're a monster. A damn demon straight from the flames of Hell." Rearing back her arm, she slapped my brother with every ounce of strength she had in her. Trevor took a stumbling step back, his cheek scarlet where she struck him.

Trevor's shocked expression shifted into a sneer, and he took a step forward, lording over her intimidatingly. "Tell your fuckin' faggot son I said hi." The corner of his lip curled higher. "Oh, wait. You can't, can you? He's on a bus right now, and you ain't ever going to see him again. Your husband will see to it. We talked about it when I called and told him what happened." He turned his gaze to me. "He's dead to them. Pastor Fox said so." Cocking his head to the side, he smirked at her. "Are you proud of yourself, Cat? Coming over to bully my family because you're too much of a fucking coward to get off your fat ass and go find your son?" He arched an eyebrow. "Nice handprint. It's good to know there's at least one man around these parts who knows how to keep his woman in line."

Mrs. Fox looked like she was ready to end his life, and so did I. I launched off the bed and rushed forward, shoving Trevor into the hallway wall. He was so much bigger than me, I barely made an impact at all. As I I dug my fingernails into his chest as deeply as I could get them, he laughed like it was all a joke.

"You don't want to do this, Grayson."

"Fuck you!" The word felt foreign on my tongue. I never swore, but he dragged the word out of me, and once it was out, I couldn't stop. "Sister Fox is right. You're a goddamn demon, and I hope when all this is over you get just as much as you gave to Kent. I hope someone crushes everything you love and—" I stopped myself, watching in shock as he balled a fist and lifted it. It crashed against my face, sending sharp, unrelenting pain spreading across my cheek and nose. He punched me. He actually hit me.

The blow sent me stumbling back and falling against the floor. My head hit the wall and a picture frame fell, crashing down on me; glass shattered and, my head throbbed with dull pain.

Trevor turned and glared at Sister Fox, whispering, "If you don't get the fuck out of this house, I'll do the same to you. Never come back here. Don't look at my brother again. Don't speak to him. You and your faggot son can stay the fuck away from my family."

Sister Fox was trembling, and whether it was from fear or anger, I couldn't be sure. "If you think threatening to hit me is going to make me cower down, you've got another thing coming. I've been married to Joel Fox since I was eighteen. I wrote the book, sugar." Her hands shook as she took a defiant step forward. "God damn you, Trevor Collins. God damn you straight to Hell."

Footsteps reverberated up the stairwell, then my mother was in front of us, staring down at me in horror.

"What happened?" Momma asked. She knelt beside me, taking a handkerchief out of her pocket and placing it against my nose. "Why is your nose bleeding?" I couldn't get a word out. I tried. Really, I did, but I couldn't make my mouth work.

"She just ran up here and punched him," Trevor said, feigning sympathy as he ran his fingers through my hair. He was trying to come across as soothing to hide the truth from Momma. When his hand rested against the back of my head—out of Momma's line of sight—he curled his fingers, gripping my hair and pulling as hard as he could without being noticed. "Isn't that right, Grayson?"

My face was aching from where he'd hit me, and the pull he had on my hair felt like someone was ripping each hair out, strand by strand. I just wanted the pain to stop. I wanted everything to stop.

"Yes," I cried out, hating Trevor for forcing me to hurt Sister Fox again, and hating myself even more for going along with it.

To my horror, I watched as Momma glared at Sister Fox, raised her hand, and slapped her across the face. "You get the hell out of my house. If you think you can come in here and assault my son just because you couldn't control your boy, you're in for a rude awakening."

Sister Fox stared down at me, holding her cheek, looking shell-shocked. I opened my mouth to argue in her defense, but with Momma distracted, Trevor leaned in, bringing his mouth to my ear.

"Tell her to leave," he whispered, his voice hitting like poisoned darts. "Tell her to get the fuck out, or I swear to God, Grayson, I'll drag your ass to the lake and give you the same treatment I gave your queer boyfriend."

I stared into Sister Fox's eyes, tears dripping down my cheek. "Go," I choked out, the words feeling like a betrayal. "Get out. Just leave, Sister Fox."

She let go of her cheek, her hand falling to her side, and the look she gave me sent a chill down my spine. It wasn't anger or rage or devastation. It was disappointment. Resignation. The realization that we both just lost the most important person in our lives, and we could never get him back.

She nodded, but her eyes didn't leave mine. "I'll pray for you, sweetie." With her back to me, she paused. "I don't have time to take care of Abe. Not with Kent gone." That was a flat-out lie. Sister Fox had nothing but time on her hands. "I know you'e close with him'" She sniffled. "Would you like to have him, Gray?"

I had to hold back a sob. I couldn't have Kent, but I could still have a relic of the life we shared. A memento of who we were supposed to be.

I didn't give Trevor or Momma a chance to object. "Yes!"

"I'll bring him by tomorrow."

***

Later that night, just a few minutes past midnight, my bedroom door creaked open. I didn't need to look up to know it was him. He stood over me like he was God staring down at his creation, prepared to send a flood to wash the world clean.

I didn't fight it. There was no use.

"It's all going,'" he said matter-of-factly.

I was numb. It was like I was watching it happen to someone else. I stood by the door as he rummaged through my things, collecting relics of my life with Kent. An old sweatshirt that still smelled like him. A VHS tape I was planning on giving him for his birthday. Trevor left no space untouched as he searched out my hidden history with the boy I loved. By the end, he had an armful of Kent's belongings and a small bag of mementos I hoped might get me through losing both Kent and the rainbow-colored sparkle in my heart.

As Trevor led me through the hall, down the stairs, and toward the kitchen, I held onto the few things he was allowing me to carry. A picture of us I was going to try my hardest to hide away. A friendship bracelet Kent made. Just for me. A poorly drawn doodle of the Spice Girls he gave me, trying to get me to like them as much as him. Trevor didn't stop walking until we were out back, behind the barn.

It was really happening. I was going to lose every trace of what we shared. All I'd have left would be a picture. The most influential man in my life, reduced to grainy pixels.

Please don't forget me.

Trevor must have been planning it for a while, because there was already a burn barrel set up with wood inside and the same canister of gas he used to scare Kent at the lake.

I knew what was coming next, and I hated him for it. I probably should have fought him, but he'd already taken so much from me. What was the point? All it would earn me was a black eye or another bloody nose, and a heart even more broken than the one I already had.

As he poured gas into the barrel, I managed to sneak the old picture of us together—of Two-liter and his Half-pint—beneath my shorts, into my underwear. If Trevor found it, he'd probably smack me around again, but I was long past caring.

Trevor lit a match and let it fall, sending our history skyward like a beacon. For a second, I hoped God might see it and take me home. That He knew how bad I was hurting, and He would show mercy. I closed my eyes, imagining walking through those pearly gates. There would be floors of marble with golden pathways leading up to His throne. He'd be sitting up there, His arms held open to welcome me home.

"Grayson," He would say, His voice loud and filled with thunder. *"Well done, my child,"* He would say, and I'd know He meant it. That I'd passed His test.

Trevor pointed at the barrel. "Toss the rest in there. All of it."

I kept my eyes on him as I did it. It felt like it was my only way of standing my ground. That if I stared deep enough into his eyes, I might pierce his soul. Maybe it could crack some of thw concrete he slathered around his heart. I didn't know if it was possible to hate anyone more than I hated him.

When I got back to my room, I pulled the picture of us out of my underwear and stared at the smiling face of the man I loved. In the picture, we were happy. We radiated love. Through his wet eyes and tear-streaked cheeks, Kent Fox was staring at me like I'd just given him the world. Maybe I had. Maybe by letting him go, I gave him some form of peace. An escape from this God-forsaken city and its God-damned people. In Dallas, he could burn bright, like a lighthouse in the dead of night. Maybe one day his light could guide me back to him.

There was a framed picture of Jesus on my nightstand. I didn't have a whole lot to say to Jesus or God at the moment, so I turned it over and opened the tabs holding the cardboard backing in place. I removed the picture of Jesus, because he hadn't done anything to help when I was in need. I knew I couldn't keep the photo of Kent and me in the open—not in its current state, at least—so I did the only thing I could.

I stared down at Kent's lovestruck face, and I said goodbye to the boy with tangled curls.

"I love you," I whispered, low enough so only God could hear. "Be safe for me, Half-pint." I stroked his cheek in the photo. "Be happy." I brought the picture to my lips and gave him one last kiss. "Come home to me one day. I'll wait forever if I have to."

I folded the edge of the picture back, tucking Kent away. Out of sight, but never out of mind. It was my only way of keeping him safe. Keeping him hidden from prying eyes that would look upon him with shame. As I buried Kent Fox behind the cardboard, I buried a part of myself, as well. The part I could never let them see.

The spark that burned beautiful, just for him.

NOT
The End

CONTINUE KENT & GRAY'S STORY IN
We Burn Beautiful

A note from Lance

Yeah. That was rough. This one hurt to write. Gray's book has been a labor of love. I can't thank you enough for reading. I hope it was an enjoyable ride. If you're feeling heartbroken, now's the perfect time for a We Burn Beautiful reread.

If you enjoyed Gray's story, I would be eternally grateful if you could leave a review.

If you need a little more Kent and Gray in your lives (and, I mean, honestly, who doesn't?) I have three short stories told from Gray's POV available in my Facebook reader group, Lance Lansdale's Library.

Sorry if I made you cry.

For more about me
FOLLOW ME ON SOCIAL MEDIA

INSTAGRAM	@LANCETASTIK (WITH A K)
FACEBOOK	@LANCETASTIC
BLUESKY	@LANCETASTIC
FACEBOOK GROUP	LANCE LANSDALE'S LIBRARY

LANCELANSDALE.COM

Made in United States
Cleveland, OH
30 March 2025